DESTINED
To Trust in Love

Dennison Sisters · Book Three
LOIS CURRAN

Cover Design – Jaycee DeLorenzo
Publishing Coordinator – Sharon Kizziah-Holmes

Paperback-Press
an imprint of A & S Publishing
Paperback Press, LLC.

ISBN -13: 978-1-960499-24-0

DEDICATION

Charla Baker, lifelong BFF, and final proofreader
extraordinaire.

ACKNOWLEDGMENTS

I never want to fail to thank God for always walking beside me.

A special shout out to my incredible sons who encourage and support me in my writing adventures. Thank you, Kenny, Lon and Jason Waterman.

Thanks to my good friends and authors, Shirley McCann, and Kathy Garnsey who edit my manuscripts.

To Jaycee DeLorenzo, at Sweet 'N' Spicy Designs, who make my book covers express exactly what I want to reveal. She is amazing.

And last but not least, a special thank you to my publishing coordinator, Sharon Kizziah-Holmes. Thank you for never giving up on me and for gently pushing me to be the best I can be.

CHAPTER ONE

The light of dawn seeped into Carrie Dennison's bedroom. She rubbed her bleary eyes, walked to the window and almost forgot to breathe at the beauty of Tampa's skyline. The just-risen sun shone softly on the city streets, bringing with it a flurry of early-morning activity. She watched the sunrise ripple across the grass with gold and orange while it continued to paint its spectacular hues on the sand. A hint of rain teased the air as the sky weaved a story through the delicate clouds. She loved her apartment and especially loved Tampa.

Carrie followed the rich scent of brewed coffee calling her from her pre-set Keurig K-Duo, then slipped onto a stool at her kitchen counter. Nothing tasted better than the first cup of morning coffee. A weekend off lay ahead of her, the possibilities unlimited. She'd most likely opt for cleaning her apartment after her morning run. Then church on Sunday. Not an exciting life, but she was content.

After a mug of wake-me-up and a croissant drizzled with a dab of honey, she dressed in her work-out shorts and top, stuffed a bottled water into her bag, then stepped through the back door.

A brisk late March breeze tickled the back of her neck and pulled up her short ponytail. The western half of the sky, where the weather change came from, darkened quickly. Nimbus clouds gathered; a deepening grey tinged with soft black at the fringe. She could smell the water hanging in the air and feel its dampness on her cheek. A storm was coming, but she figured she'd be back home before it hit. Over the years, she'd learned Florida could brew up a thunderstorm quickly, then end it just as fast.

Her feet scampered along the sidewalk at a steady pace. Six blocks from her apartment complex, at the park, she dropped her tote on a bench. She did a few stretches then started out at a nice, easy jog, breathing in the cool morning air, allowing it to fill her lungs as she pounded the trail that butted up against the palm trees behind the community center.

When her muscles loosened, she lengthened her stride and began to run. Several familiar fellow joggers waved or greeted her. She waved back but never broke her stride. Faster she went, pumping her arms, enjoying the freedom, the release from physical effort. She ran completely around the perimeter of the park, then turned toward the interior, zigzagging around the palms. Her heart pounded and the wind whistled in her ears.

Carrie's sisters had taught her the enjoyment and benefit of outdoor exercise. A treadmill had its use, but there was nothing like the great outdoors to stimulate your dopamine and serotonin levels. A better mood elevator than the Fluoxetine her doctor had prescribed several months ago. She had only taken the anti-depressant one month, then never refilled the prescription. It made her too draggy.

After jogging four miles, she slowed and walked a couple times around the track to cool down. Her breathing returned to normal by the time she flopped down on the park bench. She pulled a towel from her bag and wiped her face and neck, then opened the water and took a long drink from the bottle.

Running always helped her focus, helped her think through any issues that troubled her before they had a chance to blow up in her face and become too big to manage. Today she focused on her ex-boyfriend, Jeff. How, out of the blue, he'd called her last night and asked her to meet him, just to talk, he'd said. She had flat out declined, determined not to let his magnetism overpower her common sense. Not anymore. It had taken her too long to get over him. She was not going to let him worm his way back into her heart.

Jeff's features flashed through her mind and she tamped down the urge to cry. She'd spent more time crying over him than she'd want to admit. She frowned, adjusted her position, took another pull from the bottled water and screwed on the cap. She thought she was over the strong bursts of pain that could unexpectedly roll over her. Okay, so she'd thought wrong. At least the episodes didn't paralyze her anymore. She sighed then headed toward her car.

Had she done the right thing? Maybe she should have agreed to talk to him, just to find out what was going on in his life.

I can't be curious. I cannot open that door again. I can't fall back into something that I worked so hard to get over.

Out of nowhere, an oversized all black Labrador Retriever whizzed right at her; his eyes aimed upward on an air-born Frisbee.

"Hey, watch out," she shouted and twisted to the side, but not in time. The huge dog plowed into her, and knocked her hard into the grass. The shock rattled through her, bounced her flat on her back, breathless. The massive canine raced past her, never looking back. She watched the mutt hurl over a bench then catch the frisbee in mid-air.

Embarrassment exploded throughout her body.

"Woah, what do we have here?" A buttery warm baritone belted out. "Looks like a woman in need."

A face peered down at her and she could make out a granite hard jaw and intense, shadowed eyes. He was tall. Really tall. And with those broad shoulders he looked like a linebacker. He was dressed in an unbuttoned red-and-black plaid shirt over a black tank top, distressed jean shorts and black Reeboks. His lopsided smile made her belly flip in ways it hadn't done in longer than she cared to admit.

Her thoughts swirled so wildly she had trouble pinning them down. She'd encountered his type before, sadly enough, and that made her raw heart ache. Romance had been hard on it.

"No. Correct that. A very pretty girl."

She noticed he had a kind smile, one that made his eyes crinkle slightly in the corners.

Carrie feigned humor. "Did anybody get the license of that dog?" She tried to sit up, but the stranger threw up a hand, motioned her to stay put.

"I was watching. He never knew he hit you. Neither did the kid with him." The man glanced over his shoulder then back again. "They're long gone."

Carrie wiggled her toes. A pain shot across her foot and radiated to her knee. She hoped she hadn't broken anything, and if Mr. Scrumptious would give her some room, she could assess herself without an audience. After all, as a nurse, she felt more than qualified to gauge her condition. No need for the handsome stranger to trouble himself.

"Looks like you took a pretty bad spill."

To her surprise he lowered himself to the ground beside her, then wiped hair back from her face. His touch was soft, gentle, sending a flutter through her stomach. Then he focused his attention to her foot, carefully caressing the skin while he moved her foot in a circular motion.

"No obvious break. Hopefully not even a sprain."

She tried to nod, but lying flat on her back kind of hindered the movement.

"You most likely just twisted your ankle and

stretched the ligaments beyond the usual point. It's as painful as a sprain, but unlike a sprain, it will feel better quickly. However, you need to keep an eye on it."

Who was this guy? How did he know so much about injuries?

"If it doesn't feel better in a couple days, you probably need to see your physician."

"Will do."

"Did you hit your head when you fell?"

"No. I don't think so. It happened so fast." Her head felt fine. Maybe she'd landed on her heart, the way it pounded. He looked so handsome, squatted beside her in the grass, eyebrows knitted together over cobalt blue eyes. He was all business and that impressed her. "I'm not hurt. I twisted my ankle when I went down. Nothing more."

"Humor me."

Heat rushed to her cheeks when she met his gaze. Her breath heaved, and her heart pumped so viciously against her chest she was terrified he could see it too. What was it about this stranger— she didn't even know his name—that ignited such a reaction?

When he slipped a rock-hard arm under her shoulder and helped her sit up, she caught a whiff of soap and sweat, and on him the scent worked. She turned her head so she was inches from his face. He had blond hair with a hint of wave. Executive Contour cut she'd guess. A bit like a Hard Part Pompadour, but without the hard part and with considerably more length on the sides and back so she couldn't see the scalp. With the bluest eyes she'd ever run across, he looked every inch like Prince Charming.

Good thing she was smart enough to know better. Prince Charmings only existed in fairy tales. And though her heart squeezed with wishful thoughts, she did her best to ignore them. "My foot is fine. See?" Though it hurt when she moved her toes, she ignored the pain. She needed to put distance between her and this man that made her remember things she ought to forget. She needed to regain her equilibrium. He was far too easy to look at. And the way his eyes locked on her had become far too personal.

"Here, lean on me."

He gently tugged her to her feet and wrapped an arm around her shoulder, helping her hop three feet to a bench. When she plopped down, he lifted her foot and gave it a once over again.

"Doesn't appear to be broken. Like I said, hopefully it's not a nasty sprain."

"I'm fine, really." Carrie wanted this to be over. Such a fuss from a man she'd never laid eyes on before. His focus on her was steady and direct, and she could feel her heart beating double time in her chest. How was he able to consume her like he did with nothing more than a gaze?

Just then big drops of rain pelted down from a frenzied sky. She threw her arms over her hair to no avail.

"Here, take this." He pulled off his jacket and draped it over her head. "Let's get you to your car before you're drenched."

"I didn't drive. I walked."

"Okay, then let's get you to my car."

Carrie allowed him to gather her close and hustle her to a white Jeep Wrangler. He opened the passenger door, helped her in, then ran to the other side of the car.

"I'm sorry about all this. I'm sure you have better things to do than drive me home."

"Nope. I'd just finished my run when I noticed the dog in the process of mowing you down. Couldn't leave a lady in distress." He tossed her a wink. "I'm Kent Acuff. What's your name?"

"Carrie." She eyed him cautiously and couldn't help it, she liked what she saw.

"Well, good to meet you, Carrie." He backed out of the park. "Now, which way?"

She pointed left. "I just live a few blocks from here. In the Hensley Apartments."

"Just keep pointing. I'm not familiar with Tampa."

"Oh. Are you new in town?"

"Uh huh. I just moved to Tampa last week from Kansas City. I start work Monday at the hospital."

"Of course." A light flipped on inside of her head. "You're the new CEO at Tampa General. I knew the name sounded familiar. But you look so…"

"Young?"

He laughed, low and throaty. The sound of his amusement made her smile.

"I'm twenty-eight. How old do you think I need to be for that position?"

She chuckled. "Sorry, I didn't mean to imply…"

"No problem. I get that all the time."

She pointed him toward Ellis Avenue and he turned right.

"Do you work at the hospital?"

"Uh huh. Trauma Surgery Unit."

"Registered Nurse?

"Yes."

"You're not planning to work today, I hope." His brows pulled together while he glanced at her foot. "You need to go easy on that for a while."

"This is my weekend off."

"That's good. You can stay off your foot a couple days, let it heal and prevent further injury. Be sure and keep it elevated."

"Yeah, I will." She pointed at Oaklawn Street and he made the turn. "Third apartment down, bottom floor."

He pulled in the parking area and helped her up the sidewalk, but she didn't really need his help. Already her foot felt better. Or was it the company?

"Well, thanks, Kent. I guess I'll be seeing you around the hospital."

He nodded. "That you will."

She keyed open her door and stepped across the threshold, then turned and said goodbye.

"So long, beautiful." He gave her a wide grin and a one- fingered salute.

She stood out of sight inside the entryway and tucked her hair behind her ear. Pulling in a long breath, she watched the handsome stranger jaunt down the sidewalk to his car. He's definitely eye candy, she thought.

* * *

Kent Acuff slid into his Jeep Wrangler and started the engine. He glanced over his shoulder to steal one last peek at the attractive lady who had taken his breath. She was long gone. He chided himself for thinking maybe she'd been a little interested in him. He was sure he hadn't impressed her with his overly-protective concern. Women liked macho guys. Not medical oriented nerds who zoomed in on the physical ailments. When he'd seen her take the tumble, he'd thought for sure she was hurt. Instinct kicked in and he shifted gears to protector mode. He couldn't deny it, he'd always been a fixer.

He looked forward to seeing her at the hospital. Hopefully they could form a friendship. Nothing more, he thought. Starting a relationship with a subordinate was not a good idea.

Still, he couldn't deny the instant attraction he'd felt for her.

After he'd driven the couple miles to the condo he'd rented last week, he realized he didn't live that far from Carrie. He pulled into the parking garage, parked in one of the two spaces assigned to him and headed to his front door.

His condo, located on the second floor, consisted of one bedroom and one bath with access to a backyard deck that faced the garden. A great view. Great place to have his morning coffee. Great place to have evening coffee with Carrie. He shook his head and rebuked thoughts of the pretty little nurse and concentrated on things at hand.

After he showered, he pulled lunch meat from

the fridge and opened a loaf of bread, then slathered two slices with mayo and mustard. Chips and sweet tea topped off his early lunch. He scooted the paper plate aside and poured over the info he'd received from the hospital which included an attached map of the facility. The main hospital campus, located on Davis Islands was licensed for 1,040 beds. Eight thousand team members. The total patient revenue was almost nine and a half billion dollars.

Before he'd taken the position as CEO, he'd learned Tampa General was the region's first and largest teaching hospital, and more than 700 residents were assigned to the facility for specialty training. He sucked in a breath when he realized he'd have situations ahead of him that would test his competence, but he'd never backed away from a challenge.

CHAPTER TWO

When the doorbell rang Saturday afternoon, Carrie hopped on one foot to the front door, opened it, and let her oldest sister and two kiddos come in.

"Hey Abby, what are you doing here?"

"I wanted to stop by and check on you." Abby's eyes grew round and drifted downward to Carrie's foot. "Way to go Boo Boo."

"Wasn't my fault. I was attacked by a killer dog." Her ankle still smarted but it already felt better. Kent was spot on with his diagnosis.

Carrie reached for three-year-old Adam and hoisted him on her hip. She balanced herself on one foot with the injured foot gently touching the floor. Though the ankle felt much better, she continued to baby it. She didn't want to skip work Monday and miss the chance of maybe seeing Mr. Hunk again.

"Yeah, right," Abby said. "Blame an innocent animal."

Her sister squatted, then ran gentle fingers over Carrie's swollen ankle.

"Truth. That dog knocked the air out of me." Carrie took her five-year-old niece's hand and led her to the couch.

"Aunt Boo Boo got a boo boo." Amanda sing-songed, 'I've got a boo-boo' in her sweet rendition of the *Boo Boo Song.*

"It's gonna be okay little girl." Carrie pushed Amanda's hair off her forehead, then gave the bare spot a big kiss.

She wondered if Kent had the urge to kiss her forehead when he'd gently tucked her damp hair away from her face.

Amanda giggled, bringing Carrie back to the present.

"Okay," Abby said. "I want details on the hunk that came to your rescue."

Carrie chuckled. "He was definitely eye-candy. Very nice too. Turns out he's the new CEO at the hospital."

"No way."

"Yes. Way."

"At Tampa General? Where you work?"

"Yes. Where I work."

Abby let out a wolf whistle, then said, "You know how to pick your accidents."

"Not really. I was totally embarrassed. How would you like to meet someone for the first time flat on your back, wind knocked out of your body?"

"Wouldn't mind at all if I ended up snagging the

guy."

"He's gonna be my boss. The big boss. Emphasis on big." Carrie stepped into the kitchen, and returned in a few minutes with a tray of sugar cookies, two fruit juice jugs for the littles, and a coffee for her sister.

"I can't wait to see him."

"Stop by the hospital. Maybe I can point him out."

Carrie watched her sister gobble down a sugar cookie. Abby had the perfect life. A husband that adored her. Two precious children – a daughter and a son – beautiful and healthy. She worked from home so she not only had a career, she could be a full-time mother as well. Things had not always been so perfect for her. She'd had her share of disappointment and heartbreak. But when she'd met Sam and finally trusted him enough to open her heart and let him in, things turned around for her.

"I assume he's single."

"He wasn't wearing a ring. Didn't mention a wife or family."

"And you made a point to check out his ring finger. Hmmm." Abby tapped the side of her face with her finger and looked thoughtful.

"I just happened to notice." Carrie playfully poked her sister's shoulder. "Don't make something out of nothing."

"Well, we'll just see how this plays out." Abby reached for another cookie, then added, "So, tell me what Jeff wanted when he called you."

"At first he just chit-chatted for a couple minutes like he used to do. He acted like we'd never broken up." Carrie tossed her hands in the air. "Then out of nowhere he said he missed seeing me. Missed our time together. Said he'd like to meet me for lunch or coffee and catch up."

"Oh, good grief! What a player. What did you say?"

"Of course I gave him a negative reply and when he came back with, 'Just to talk,' I told him we didn't have anything else to discuss. And he dropped it. He sounded put out though."

"Oh poor baby." Abby's eyebrows drew together. "I can't believe he had the nerve to even call you after the shabby way he treated you."

Carrie shrugged. "I'll admit I was tempted to meet with him. It's hard to quit loving someone you've loved for most of your life."

"I'm proud of you," Abby said. "You did good."

I'm proud of me too, Carrie thought. *I never thought I'd be able to say no to him.* She'd loved him since she was sixteen years old. Life without Jeff always felt like life without breath. She felt certain he'd loved her at one time also. College changed all that. They'd decided to see other people while they attended different colleges and that did it for Jeff. He'd discovered he liked being with other girls, lots of other girls. And he doted on the attention.

Not her. She'd never wanted to be with anyone but Jeff.

"Are you still with me...?"

Abby's voice brought her out of her reverie.

"I'm here." Carrie shook her head. "Just allowing myself a moment to remember how much

I loved Jeff. But just a moment. I'm okay now. I promise."

"I know you are. You've come a long way since Jeff. . ."

"Dumped me?" Carrie blew out a sigh. "It's okay to say it. That's exactly what he did."

"You're so much better off without him. I hope you know that."

"I do."

Carrie knew both of her siblings understood how a failed relationship cut deeply. Rejection and heartbreak were never easy to get through.

"We are definitely survivors. A little scarred from the battle, but we are still standing." Carrie reached for her sister's hand, took it, and pulled her in for a long hug.

The Dennison sisters always come out on top.

CHAPTER THREE

Monday morning Kent headed to Tampa General to meet with Ed Styles, the previous CEO who planned to stay on for two weeks until Kent felt comfortable. Fortunately for Kent, Ed, a fifteen-year employee, decided it was time to retire and Kent was more than ready to take the plunge. He knew the hospital strived to create a culture of success and high-quality healthcare for patients, and he planned to uphold the vision. Diving into a leadership position, he felt certain he could create a positive and productive culture, setting and following standards for operational excellence. Yes, it was time to stretch his wings and settle into a forever job. Tampa was a good choice and he'd like it here. Especially if Carrie remained in the picture.

Ed met him in the reception area of his office.

"Good morning, Kent. It's good to have you on board."

"I'm happy to join the force."

Ed motioned to the lady behind the reception desk. "This is my. . . well, soon to be your secretary, Sheila."

"Nice to meet you, Sheila."

The secretary stood, extended her hand. "I look forward to working with you, Mr. Acuff."

Kent accepted her gesture. "Please call me Kent."

She nodded then returned to her chair.

He'd planned to spend Monday shadowing his mentor, gaining insight into Ed's day-to-day routine. But Kent was surprised when, after receiving an urgent phone call, Ed began his workday in the conference room with department directors. Several staff had contracted flu-like symptoms, leaving the units short-staffed. After the back-and-forth conversations continued for several minutes, a solution was reached. Call in the part-time, prn employees. Also notify the emergency volunteers to be on stand-by.

Kent tagged along with his mentor when Ed was summoned to Outpatient Services. Influenza ran rampant in the community and the department had nearly exhausted their flu vaccine supply due to an overabundance of patients flooding into the section, seeking preventative immunizations.

Kent smiled when Ed reached in his pocket, pulled out his cell and punched in a number.

"Sheila, call Sanofi and order 500 flu shots, stat," Ed said.

"I'm amazed you ever make it to your office." Kent rubbed his jaw. "Your day appears to be one interruption after another."

"Sometimes." Ed chuckled. "I'm thankful I can be flexible."

"I imagine."

"One good thing about Tampa General is the united belief that we're all in this together."

Since Ed didn't appear to expect a response, Kent only nodded and followed him to the first item listed on his morning agenda, that ended up being the third.

"I always aim for a morning meeting with the executive secretary to go over the agenda for the day. Sometimes it happens, sometimes it doesn't. Sheila is used to going with the flow. If an emergency arises, like this morning, she accommodates for it. You will find that Sheila will be your right hand." He laughed. "Sometimes she's been my left hand also."

* * *

Stepping out of the shower at six o'clock Monday morning, Carrie was pleasantly surprised at how good her ankle felt. Hardly any discomfort and minimal edema. She was eager to get to work, with thoughts of Kent Acuff forefront in her mind. She wondered if she'd run into the new, handsome CEO who had gallantly rescued her in the park. She remembered his gentle touch. His amazing blue eyes that seemed to bore right through her.

Carrie looked down at her watch and realized

she'd spent too much time daydreaming. Slipping into her azure blue scrubs, she dressed quickly then pulled on her new white Gales nursing shoes. She glanced at her full-length mirror image. She looked like the early pictures she'd seen of her father, wideset brown eyes with a hint of amber if the light was just right. Brunette hair that she pulled back into a tight bun at the nape of her neck for work. The only difference, Dad stood six-foot-three inches tall, compared to her petite five-foot-two.

Satisfied with her appearance, she removed her phone from the charger and brought it to the kitchen, then put a frozen bagel in the toaster and poured a cup of coffee. She tapped the phone to wake it up. A quick glance revealed a couple missed calls from unfamiliar numbers which she deleted. When her bagel popped up, she ate standing at the kitchen counter. No time to dawdle this morning.

A swipe with a wet sponge over the kitchen counter, the cup rinsed and placed in the dishwasher, and she headed to her car for the short drive to work.

"Good morning." The security officer's smile broadened from ear to ear.

"Good morning." Carrie walked through the weapons screening unit at the main entrance of Tampa General.

A succession of threats had led to a policy change for all entrances to the hospital. Everyone, employees and visitors, had to go through the security line. No exceptions.

She entered the elevator and pushed the number four button. When it stopped and the door slid open, she exited and made a bee-line to the nursing station. The Trauma Surgery Unit's counter was occupied by the lone overnight ward clerk. The rest of the night shift were winding down, ready to turn the unit over to the day shift.

True to her routine, Carrie arrived before her co-workers. She wanted a chance to check out admission notes before shift report started. In high school and college, she had been very casual about arriving on time. When a class was taught in a lecture hall, she would often slink into a seat in the back row to avoid the attention of the professor. Her experience with her nursing clinicals had made her the opposite. She was now not only punctual; she always arrived early for all appointments.

She smiled at the clerk, then pulled the admissions file and flipped it open.

"Hey, Carrie." Brenda, her nurse supervisor and friend, stepped behind the counter. "Did you have a nice weekend?"

"I did, other than one very minor accident Saturday morning." Carrie smiled at her friend. Brenda looked to be mid-forties with stylish brown hair, cut short at the nape of her neck, and longer layers around her face. She'd been employed at Tampa General for fifteen years. She took the supervisor position over the Trauma Surgery Unit five years ago.

"Accident?" Brenda asked.

"I took a tumble and had an aggravated ankle for a day and a half."

"Bummer." Brenda's eyes widened. "Hope it's better."

Carrie nodded while she flipped through the night report.

Two more of the staff nurses reported for duty. Gwen, the newest graduate of the RNs, was maybe a couple years younger than Carrie, which would make her twenty-three. A real go-getter, she wanted to learn all she could cram into a day's worth of nursing care. Linda, her opposite, had worked on the unit five years and knew it like the back of her hand. Both were excellent nurses and enjoyable to work with.

"Have you guys seen the new CEO yet?" Gwen's eyebrows bounced up and down. "He's got to be the best-looking specimen of a man I've ever laid eyes on."

Gwen was attractive but had the slightest hint of peach fuzz on her face that seriously needed to be waxed. Thankfully she was a blonde and the facial hair was light. It was only emphasized when she stood in direct sunlight.

"Oh yeah. I nearly fainted when I first got a glimpse of him. I'd love to get my hands around those biceps." Linda tapped a palm on her chest. "Be still my heart."

Linda was 28. Carrie knew because they'd just had cake and ice cream for her birthday in the breakroom last week and they'd arranged twenty-eight candles on her cake. Same age as Kent, Carrie thought. Linda had a husband and little girl, but she never failed to express her opinion regarding the good looks of a member of the opposite sex.

"You girls." Brenda laughed and shook her head. "I agree, he's a looker. And he's as nice as he is gorgeous. He met with the department supervisors. Just to get to know us, he said."

"Wish I could have sat in on that meeting." Linda ran her tongue over her lower lip.

"Actually, I had a one-on-one meeting with him." Carrie fanned her face with her hand.

"You what?" Brenda's jaw dropped an inch.

"You wish." Gwen shook her head, and laughed. "In your dreams, girlfriend."

Linda cocked her head to the side. "No way."

"Well let me tell you. . ." Carrie took the next few minutes to relate the day in the park when the lab flew into her.

"Oh my gosh!" Gwen's green eyes grew wide. "I'd let a horse mow me down if it meant I could have his arms around me."

"I'll admit, it was kinda nice. But honestly, I was so embarrassed. I must have looked a mess. Flat on my back in the grass. No makeup. Hair pulled back. And I'm sure I was sweaty. I'd jogged four miles."

Just then the night nurse walked behind the counter, took her position at the nursing station, and reported the night's new admissions before moving on to the routine patients.

Carrie's morning flew by in a blur of patient care. She'd had specialty training that qualified her to work on the 24-bed Trauma Surgery Unit, and she loved her job. She cared for a diversity of patients who had suffered complex traumatic injuries that included multiple fractures, traumatic brain injuries, internal injuries and lacerations, along with general surgery, hepatology and urology issues. Due to the complex nature of these injuries, the Trauma Surgery staff had been trained to provide skilled nursing care of chest tubes, tracheostomies, multiple drains, VACs, colostomies, ileostomies and complex wound care. When she signed on at Tampa General, she'd been given the choice to work NICU or the Trauma Surgery Unit, and she opted for the unit because she desired the diversity of patient care she would be able to provide. She had worked here three years and never regretted her decision.

Footsteps clicked in the hall, then a baritone 'good morning' pulled her out of her reverie.

She turned and looked into the gorgeous face of Kent Acuff. His piercing blue eyes and luscious blond hair combined with an athletic build suggested an air of authority that caused her to hitch in a breath. Dressed in a navy-blue suit with a red and light blue striped tie, he looked even more handsome than he had in the park. Something about a man in a suit got to her every time. Suddenly her mouth felt dry. She'd give anything for a big sip of water.

"Good morning." Carrie swallowed hard.

"Good morning, Carrie. How's the ankle?"

"Just fine." Carrie felt the blood draining out of her head while she watched him bend down and give her ankle an assessment. She was dizzy, rooted in place. She searched for words, wanted to keep the conversation moving forward. "What do you think of our hospital?"

"Actually it isn't that different than Kansas City General."

Carrie nodded and tried not to stare at the

powerful muscles in his shoulders. She was sure if she googled deltoids it would pull up Kent's name.

"And Ed has been great showing me the ropes."

"Ed is a sweetheart. I know he's looking forward to retirement."

"He is. Said him and his wife plan to travel."

"That sounds like Ed."

"He did share with me that he's going to miss it here at Tampa General." Kent tilted his head to the side. "From the way he talks, he really liked working here."

"I'm sure you will like it here too." Carrie felt her face turn hot. What a lame thing to say.

"I know I will." He gave her a quick wink.

His intense gaze spoke louder than his words, and if she was any judge of character, he just sent her a message. She hoped she'd read it correctly.

"I need you to sign off on Mrs. B in room 410...." Brenda nudged her.

"I won't keep you." Kent smiled, tossed her another wink, and turned on his heel. "See you around."

His lopsided smile made her stomach flutter in ways it hadn't done in longer than she cared to admit.

When she stepped behind the nurse's station, her co-workers eyed her while she gathered an iPad.

"Wow you really are chummy with the new CEO." Brenda tossed her friend a playful grin.

"All thanks to an overgrown black lab that mowed me down." Carrie chewed her lower lip while she entered her passcode into the iPad, and scrolled to Mrs. Benton's chart.

"Lucky you." Linda wrinkled her nose. "What I'd give to have him drive me home."

Carrie stifled a grin. An aura of friendly green jealousy surrounded her friends. Kent had made a point to approach her. But she couldn't let her head be turned by the handsome CEO. He was way too good looking for his own good. He was sure to attract every female in the hospital. Young or old. Single or married. She knew she'd have to keep her heart on guard. She did not want to end up falling for someone who'd let her down. Not again. Jeff had caused her enough pain to last a lifetime. She planned never to be in a serious relationship again. Too painful. She'd keep it simple. Dinner, a movie. Nothing serious.

She vowed she'd never let another man worm his way into her life. Done with that, she thought. Then she turned her attention to tasks at hand, concentrated on today's schedule which revealed several new surgeries. She'd take care of the post-ops. That should be her only goal. Not dwelling on the irresistible CEO with his wide shoulders and penetrating blue eyes.

But before she'd had time to check today's patients, Brenda approached her in the hallway.

"I need to deliver this information to Mr. Acuff." Brenda held up a folder. "He requested the stats from each department. This is ours."

Carrie stood quietly and eyed Brenda.

"Since you and Kent seem to have hit it off, I'm gonna give you the chance to see his office up close and personal." Brenda laughed and extended the info toward her. "Seriously, I don't have time to run these down there. Would you mind to take them?"

Carrie nodded and accepted the folder. Would she mind? What a laugh. She'd love to see the office since he'd taken over. She'd been in there a few times when Ed was CEO and had admired how he'd decorated the area.

Ed's PR team had insisted any discussion of his private life was out of bounds. Of course, Ed had implied a good CEO ignored certain do's and don'ts. She wondered how Kent would handle the PR.

CHAPTER FOUR

Carrie exited the elevator on the first floor and crossed the lobby with as much purpose in her stride as she could muster, pretending she wasn't excited about seeing Kent.

"Hello, Carrie." Sheila looked up. "How are you today?"

Seated at the administration reception desk, Sheila greeted Carrie with a smile. She was young, maybe twenty, thin with shoulder length strawberry blonde hair and green expressive eyes. Smart and always upbeat, she radiated friendliness.

"I'm good. I've got a report from Trauma Surg to give to Kent, uh, Mr. Acuff."

"It's okay to call him Kent. In fact he insists. He is really one nice guy."

Carrie wondered if Sheila might be interested in

Kent. The way her eyes smiled when she talked about him lit up her face. She glanced at the secretary's left hand to make sure Sheila still had a fiancé. She did. The engagement ring on her third finger remained in place, answering Carrie's unspoken question.

"Do you want to leave it with me? Kent is on a conference call." Sheila's eyebrows raised a fraction, her gaze shifted to the phone on the desk. "Hold on. He just finished the call."

Carrie shifted from one foot to the other while she watched Sheila walk to Kent's door. "Carrie from fourth floor is here with their unit's report."

A few beats later Kent appeared in the doorway, his biceps bulging under the starched cotton of his tailored shirt.

"Come in, Carrie."

The throaty murmur of his voice prickled over her skin every time she heard him speak.

Everything about this man was exciting, overwhelming. The way he said her name with the slightest hint of intimacy would disarm any woman who came within a ten-mile radius. Standing less than two feet from him, no wonder her pheromones were toast. He had the power to unsettle her completely.

She laid the folder on his modern black computer desk and suddenly felt at a loss for words.

"Thank you," he said.

His formal tone was deep and gravelly, containing a tiny pinch of Missouri, the combination of which was scarily mellow and pleasant.

And now he was looking at her the way someone might look at a ticking bomb. She wondered why there was a weird fluttery feeling in her chest.

"Sit for a minute if you can take a break." Kent motioned to a chair beside his desk. "I won't keep you long. I don't want to get you in trouble with your supervisor."

She turned and scanned his neatly arranged workspace before she slid into the seat. It seemed to fit him perfectly.

"I like what you've done with your office." Carrie's eyes took in the credenza placed under the window. A Keurig, 4 mugs hanging on a cup tree, and assortments of powdered cream and sweetener were arranged on a tray positioned in the middle of the table. Near the left wall a Bon Air chandelier hung above a round table with four chairs. A contemporary 3-piece bookcase sprawled on the wall behind his desk, and what she liked best was the office wall decal with a black background and white letters that said, BE THE PERSON YOU WANT TO WORK WITH.

"Thanks. I just kind of threw some things I like together." She saw his eyes scan the room. "You can probably tell I'm pretty much in to modern décor."

"I like modern too." His office scheme was completely different than Ed's. She had liked the way Ed decorated the office, but Kent's décor was by far a step ahead. "You've done a great job."

He gave her a thumbs up and leaned forward. "I'm glad you approve, Carrie." His gaze locked with hers.

Carrie's heartbeat accelerated and her breathing clogged in her lungs, making her feel like a starstruck school girl. She stood, ignoring the wobble in her knees. "Well, I better get back to the unit before they send a search party looking for me."

"I'll walk you out. I've got a meeting in the conference room in a few."

When he cupped her elbow to escort her out of the office, she felt a shock shoot up her arm, like she'd backed into an electric fence.

She let him guide her through his doorway, past Sheila's desk, into the hallway.

When she turned left to return to her floor, he gave her a two-finger salute and turned right.

"Thanks for delivering the file, Carrie. You're the best."

"You're welcome." Carrie heard the slight tremble in her voice, and by the look on Kent's face, he'd heard it too. She raced to the elevator and didn't dare turn around. If she got caught looking at him, she'd die of embarrassment.

Carrie stepped into the elevator and punched the button for her floor, trying to appease the whirlwind of idyllic thoughts that whirled like a fidget spinner in her mind. A wave of warmth climbed all the way up to her face. Shaking her head, she fought hard to regain her composure because she knew every eye would be on her when she took her position at the nurse's station. She hoped her cheeks didn't reveal how hot they felt.

* * *

Kent watched Carrie round the corner and hurry away. His gaze narrowed to the dark brown hair pulled back in a low ponytail. A ripple of reaction streaked down his spine, his senses roared to life, and a lightning strike of awareness fired through his system. There was something special about this nurse that demanded his attention.

When he walked into the empty conference room, his mind still buzzed with visions of Carrie. Her fathomless chocolate-brown eyes, with specks of amber surrounded by thick dark lashes, seemed to look right through his soul. Seeing her twice in one morning was more than Kent could have hoped for.

His mind conjured up the beautiful nurse's reaction to his earlier impromptu visit to the Trauma Surgery Unit.

When he'd approached Carrie by the nurse's station, he'd watched the change in her demeanor when she turned and saw it was him that spoke to her. A smile had blossomed on her face as recognition lit up her eyes. He smiled at the memory. He'd felt a strong urge to give her a hug, but thankfully he had managed to control his unprofessional reaction.

Then just now, to his surprise, when she'd shown up at his office, he could barely contain his elation. He wondered if she'd read the telltale signs in his eyes.

He raked a hand through his hair, unable to deny the attraction he felt for the surgery unit nurse. The fact was he was intrigued with her from the moment he'd first laid eyes on her. Something about Carrie made his pulse kick up a notch. Not only was she beautiful, she was a humble, courteous, and gentle person, as well as strong spirited while still maintaining her gentleness. And her bashful grin made her even more beautiful. And how he loved that smile.

Be careful, he warned himself. Things could get complicated if he developed a close relationship with a nurse at the hospital. He glided a hand along the smooth surface of the long executive conference table. Even if he wanted to tread cautiously where Carrie was concerned, he doubted that would be possible. He couldn't deny she was one woman he, for sure, wanted to get to know better.

The door to the conference room opened, and he watched Ed stroll through the doorway.

"Good morning, Ed."

"Morning. How'd your first solo walk-through go?"

"Great. Met the unit directors and a lot of their staff." One staff member impressed me more than the others he thought, but, of course, didn't share with his mentor the newly found infatuation he'd developed for a certain petite brunette nurse.

Kent seated himself in the oversized swivel chair next to Ed in the boardroom for his initial meeting with the directors. The seven-member hospital board would be his boss. He'd answer directly to them with any changes, decisions, and/or problems that might arise.

The board that his former CEO answered to in Kansas City could at times be demanding. Kent hoped for a board here that would be easy to get along with and easy to please. He already had ideas he wanted to implement. He wondered if this board would be open about changes from an outsider. Always the optimistic, he hoped for the best.

Thirty minutes later, meeting over, Kent had his answer to his new bosses' attitudes. They seemed reasonable, well-informed professional individuals that, like him, only wanted the best for Tampa General Hospital. Open to suggestions, they were patient-focused above all else. Just like him, he thought, as he sorted through some ideas he had tucked away in his cerebrum.

CHAPTER FIVE

Carrie opted for a late lunch break then headed to the hospital cafeteria. No wonder she was hungry, she'd skipped breakfast. Friends often asked her if she felt uncomfortable going to lunch alone. Her answer was quite the opposite. There was nothing lonely about solitude, on the contrary, it was an opportunity to gather thoughts. Plus, she was a bona fide people watcher.

Lots of complaints about hospital food not being fit to eat floated among the patients. But clients who complained most likely were on a restricted diet. She found the food served at Tampa General as good as most restaurants. Lots of choices as well.

Today she opted for a grilled chicken salad with ranch dressing and assorted fruit on the side. Tray in hand, she seated herself at an empty table near the window with a view of Hyde Park. The table opposite hers was occupied by a couple who appeared to be in their early to mid- thirties. They leaned across the table and apparently shared a secret. Newlyweds she'd guess.

"Mind if I join you?" The question pulled Carrie's attention away from the couple. She knew the voice before she turned her head to the side.

She sat up straighter. "No, I'd like that."

Kent set his tray on the table, and Carrie could not help but notice he must have a hearty appetite. Steak, baked potato, side salad, and broccoli drizzled with cheese made her salad look puny.

"I hear Ed is going to go ahead and take his retirement since he feels you already have a grasp on the ins and outs of the hospital." Carrie picked up her glass, took a small sip of sweet tea.

"Yes, he plans to leave at the end of the week. He's anxious to start his life of leisure." Kent cut into his steak and Carrie noticed it was medium well. Just like she liked.

"He speaks highly of you." Carrie forked some salad, stopped mid-air when she suddenly felt self-conscious. What if she crunched too loud?

"He's been an enormous help to me. Glad I could do my on-the-job training with him."

"Ed is a sweetheart." Carrie smiled. "He will be missed."

"I know I, for one, will miss him. He's assured me he will be available to answer any questions I may have in the future."

"That's Ed, for sure. Always willing to help."

Carrie glanced down at her untouched salad.

This was ridiculous, she scolded herself. If I just sit here not eating, I will look even more lame than if I crunched here and there. After all, she told herself, her chewing was much more amplified to her ears than any bystander. She put the forked bite into her mouth, and chewed as silently as she could manage. Then she glanced at Kent to see if he noticed. He didn't seem to.

After they ate in comfortable silence for a few minutes, Carrie relaxed, disregarded mastication sounds, and managed to finish her salad.

The handsome man seated across from her left not a crumb on his plate.

"Have you lived in Tampa long, Carrie?'

"Yes. Been here several years."

"I imagine you are familiar with the layout of the area then."

"Uh huh. Pretty much."

"Would you be so kind as to show me the highlights of this great city? On your day off? I am green as to where to go or what to do."

His words squeezed her heart. Was he asking her for a date? She felt heat rush to her cheeks. Why did this man have such magnetism? And why wasn't she trying to resist?

"Sure, I'd be glad to." She hoped her voice didn't reveal her nervousness.

"I'll be happy to buy your lunch at your favorite spot."

"That's a deal. I'm off weekends this month." Lucky me, she thought. Carrie was well aware the CEO always had weekends off. She rotated her days off with the other nurses in her department, snagging a month of weekends off about every three months.

"I'll pick you up at ten Saturday morning if that works for you."

"Sounds perfect."

* * *

First thing she did when she arrived home after work that evening was place a face-time call to her siblings. She wanted to see their faces when she shared her excitement with them.

When their images appeared on the screen, Carrie said, "Hey, how's it going?"

"What's up?" Abby asked.

"Yeah, are you okay?" Emily's eyes grew wide.

Carrie could hear concern in both sisters' voices.

"Nothing is wrong, I promise. Absolutely nothing. Things couldn't be better."

"So why do you sound so hyper?" Emily asked.

"I've got news. Good news. For me anyway." She laughed. Really laughed, like she hadn't done in a long time. Not since Jeff.

"Okay, spill it," Abby said.

Carrie smiled. The anticipation in her older sister's voice was obvious.

"Yeah, what's got you so excited?" Emily's tone revealed her usual impatience.

"I can barely contain myself."

Both her sisters yelled, "What?"

"I've got a date with Kent." Carrie blurted into her phone. "Can you believe that?"

"Wow. He worked fast. Must be smitten with my

little sister." Abby's smiling face filled the screen.

"I don't know about that, Abs." Carrie dropped her voice to a whisper. "But I do know I like him more every time I'm around him."

"He's lucky you fell for him. And the emphasis is on fell." Abby's voice hitched up a notch and she laughed at her own joke.

"You're too funny." Carrie pulled the ponytail holder from her hair, and shook her tresses free.

"I knew you'd find someone at work. Lots of promising possibilities in a hospital setting." Emily laughed. "And the guy my sister falls for just happens to be the top dog."

"Only the best for our baby sister." Abby's smile lit up her face.

Carrie shook her finger at the screen. "We aren't even a couple, and you two have me walking down the aisle."

"I knew you'd eventually put Jeff behind you." Emily cleared her throat. "And find someone who would actually treat you with respect."

"Me too." Abby agreed.

Carrie pulled in a breath. She sensed an 'I told you so' brewing with both sisters.

"Thanks for riding the wave with me." Carrie blew her siblings a kiss. "I really am over Jeff."

"Didn't I tell you?" Emily asked.

"Yes, Em, you told me." Carrie chuckled.

Emily always wanted to get the last word in. But that was okay. She had to admit Emily had repeated her prediction numerous times.

"You both told me. I was just too wrapped up in my pain to see it."

"So what are you going to do? Where are you going?" Abby asked.

Carrie chuckled. Her oldest sister always insisted on all the details.

"He asked me to show him the highlights of Tampa. And said he'd buy me lunch at my favorite restaurant."

"Oh my gosh." Both sisters talked at once. "How cool."

"I'll have to admit it is pretty cool." A weird flutter in Carrie's chest reminded her just how cool she thought it would be.

As customary for siblings, they wanted to know everything about her new found hunk. They pried her for details, oohing and aahing appropriately, and she was more than willing to share. Carrie thanked the Lord for her sisters every day, and she wouldn't want to do life without them. They made her complete.

An hour later, after Carrie had answered all her sister's questions, they finally wound down and said their 'good nights'.

"Talk to you soon." Carrie hit end, her heart full and thankful for a family that always shared her good times as well as the bad times.

Her siblings had been worried about her after Jeff threw her over for another woman. She had to admit, she'd been a mess, felt like the world had caved in on her. As hard as she tried, she could not pull herself from under the cloud of devastation. Thank goodness, against her protesting, her family forced her to see a psychologist. She now realized she'd been very close to falling into a clinical depression. She had lost interest in everything. All she could concentrate on was how broken she felt, how her heart ached. At that time she never believed she would ever be able to feel love for someone else. She thought she was doomed to a life alone.

Her sisters had no idea how, at her lowest point, she had begged Jeff to come back to her. Literally begged him. She wanted to feel his love again like he'd shown her in high school. She'd promised him she'd do anything to keep him in her life, told him she'd change, become the person he wanted to spend the rest of his life with. He had rejected her and told her she could never be the woman he needed. He had completely humiliated her.

CHAPTER SIX

When the phone woke Carrie Saturday morning, she bolted upright in bed. She grabbed her cell from the nightstand and saw Emily's smiling face on the screen.

"Hey, Emmy."

"You sound like you were asleep."

"I was." Carrie yawned.

"Oh, sorry."

"Don't be. I need to get up and get ready for you know who."

"I know you're excited."

"I am." Carrie dangled her legs off the side of the bed, wiggling her toes.

"You deserve this. It's time you find some real happiness."

Carrie yearned to find the kind of happiness both

her siblings had found. It hadn't been easy for either of them. They both endured past heartbreaks, but in the end, they'd found Mr. Right. Sam and Donnie were as close to perfect as any men could be.

"I just hope I don't get disappointed again. You know I don't have a very good track record where men are concerned."

"I think this time will be different for you."

"You know there was a time I thought Jeff was my forever love. And he would have been if he hadn't dumped me."

"His loss. Not yours."

"That's what I keep telling myself." Maybe it would sink in one of these days.

"You go girl. You got this."

She hoped so. Since she'd met Kent, her emotions swung back and forth like a pendulum. On one hand, she felt excited about the possibility of forming a serious relationship with the handsome CEO. But on the other hand, the fear of another heartbreak lingered. What if she opened her heart and let him in only to be crushed again?

"What are you going to wear?" Emily's question brought her back to the present.

"I'm thinking about wearing the red blousy top Abby gave me for my birthday with straight leg jeans and black kitten heels. I'll cuff the jeans and wear jewelry of course."

"Sounds perfect. Dressy enough without overdoing it. You're going to knock him off his feet."

"That's the plan." Emily chuckled.

* * *

Knowing today would be a big day – a huge day – for him, Kent had gone to bed at ten the previous night. An hour earlier than usual. But it didn't do any good. He had tossed and turned, and the speed at which his mind raced easily outweighed any chance of falling asleep. He resisted the urge to down a nighttime Tylenol. The last thing he wanted was to spend the day battling a drug-induced hangover.

He must have drifted off at some point because, when he opened his eyes and saw the normally dark room glowing with light, he realized it was Saturday. Grateful he'd finally gotten some sleep, he made an effort to calm himself; plenty of time to take care of what he needed to do before he headed to Carrie's.

Kent shuffled to the kitchen and filled a cup with strong steaming coffee, then slid into a chair. He never wanted to start the morning until he'd ingested some good strong java to clear his mind. Thoughts of the day ahead with his beautiful nurse sprayed over him like a gentle morning rain, and visions of future possibilities soared through his mind like a kaleidoscope of changing colors. His escalating attraction toward her filled him with a combination of joy and trepidation. When he was around her, he had no doubt whatsoever that he wanted to pursue a relationship. However, the fear of dating a subordinate lingered in his mind, warning him it could lead to an uncomfortable working environment.

Unfortunately, he'd slipped into a similar situation in Kansas City when he dated the CEO's private secretary. Though the attraction was one-sided, and stopped abruptly at friendship for him, she had wanted more. Much more. When he'd tried to gracefully walk away from the situation, she'd become angry and attempted, with some success, to cause him trouble. It caused an awkward workplace, to say the least.

He ran fingers through his hair, momentarily tempted to call off the outing with the tantalizing nurse. He quickly chided himself, realizing that would be downright rude. Carrie did not seem like the type who would act negatively if things did not work out. But he knew from experience that love affected people in weird ways.

Love. Why would he even consider that emotion at this early stage in the game? Because, he argued with himself, he had not felt this drawn to a woman before. Awestruck and completely baffled, he found himself lost in territory he'd never entered before. The electricity between them was absolute. He had felt the sparks from day one, and if he could read Carrie at all, she'd felt it too.

He drained his mug, scooted back from the table and headed to the shower.

Just what he needed. Muscles relaxed and thoughts modified, the hot steaming water, reduced the uncertainty he'd wrestled with over a simple date with the lovely nurse.

* * *

Carrie watched the parking lot, anxious to see Kent's jeep appear. She'd checked herself in the full-length mirror a dozen times, then finally assured herself she looked as good as she possibly could. She'd never fretted so much over how she looked. But somehow she sensed this date would be different from all others.

Finally, she spotted the familiar vehicle pull into the visitor's parking space. She stood, ran her hand down her blouse, walked to the entryway, then waited for the doorbell to chime before she pulled open the door. She didn't want to appear too anxious.

"Good morning." Carrie stepped through her doorway, letting her eyes sweep over Kent, who was definitely easy on the eye.

Dressed in a burgundy crew neck polo tucked loosely into jeans that fit him like a glove, he reeked with manly appeal. The color and style suited him. Not overly flashy, but attractive and certainly irresistible. She felt a momentary hitch in her chest as she let her eyes enjoy the gorgeous hunk that stood in front of her. He was even more good-looking today than he had looked in his suit and tie at the hospital.

"Morning, beautiful."

The warm tenor of his deep voice sluiced over her skin like warm honey. She answered him with a smile, not trusting her voice to speak just yet.

When Kent stepped toward her, she let him loop her arm in his and escort her to his Wrangler.

Situated so close to him nearly stole her breath. His woodsy scent flooded her senses, and for a split-second, she had the urge to kiss his cheek. When he looked at her and tossed her a wink, she felt chills crawl up her spine. She sucked in air to calm her nerves. They hadn't even left the parking lot, and she could feel her heart beating double time in her chest. What was it about this man? Once again she wondered how he was able to consume her like he did with nothing more than a glance. She shifted in the seat, pulled in another dose of oxygen, determined to get her emotions under control and act like she had some normality.

"Where to?" Kent turned the key in the ignition.

"Depends." Carrie tapped her chin. "Exactly what are you wanting to see?"

"I know Tampa can't be explored completely in a day. So how about you pick a spot for us to check out and we'll start there."

"Sounds like a plan."

He reached over and patted her arm. Heat replaced the chill she'd felt before. She wasn't going to make it through a whole day with him if she didn't get a grip.

"Okay. Enter GPS directions to Tampa Riverwalk. We'll start there." She felt certain he'd like the Hillsborough River that surrounded the downtown area. Tourists flogged to the area.

"Gotcha." She watched Kent push directions into his cell, then situated his phone in the dashboard mount.

"You can park in the Ybor parking garage and we'll catch the trolley to the Riverwalk."

"Okay."

For the next fifteen minutes, they made small

talk laced with lots of laughter. Carrie found Kent to have a great sense of humor. She liked serious, but she also liked a man that knew how to have fun. Laughter was good for the soul.

They passed an Arby's, a Chick-fil-A, a McDonald's, and a Dunkin' Donuts, then got off on exit 45-A. They drove through a series of beach communities, their quiet streets lined with houses, many of which were built on stilts. Each one was different from the next; modern glass affairs, old weathered clapboard with screened-in porches, and new multi-story homes with siding in colorful aluminum. Flying novelty flags with lobsters and cartoon fish dotted the sidewalks.

Seagulls scored the sky, and in time the houses grew fewer and farther apart. The landscape changed dramatically to downtown skyscrapers, offices, and large commercial buildings.

The Riverwalk, along the Hillsborough River and Garrison Channel, was a multi-use path that extended over two-and-one-half miles from Armature Works to Sparkman Wharf and connected a variety of museums, shops, restaurants, and parks. She smiled, pleased with her choice, when he nodded his approval of the scenery.

They took in the beautiful waterfront views and basked in the warm sun along the riverwalk pathway, stopping to grab a sweet tea to go at a sidewalk coffee house.

When they reached the northern end, Carrie stopped, motioned with her hand, and said, "This is Heights Market at Armature Works."

"Wow." Kent's strong jaw dropped down a

fraction.

"It's an old warehouse turned modern grub hub."

"I'm impressed."

"It has some of the yummiest food in Florida. This is where food lovers unite in a flavor explosion."

"Huge." Kent's eyes grew round.

Carrie watched him scan the area, taking in the wide continuous expanse.

"I think it's a 22,000 sq-ft industrial market if I'm not mistaken."

"This is cool. I dig the open floor plan."

"It's a food-lover's dream."

"I can tell."

"There was a lot of renovation involved here. But the project focused on keeping the historical feel of the Tampa landmark with exposed brick, skylights, original windows, and hard-wood floors."

"Looks like lots of indoor and outdoor activities." Kent cocked his head to the side.

"You could spend a week exploring this place."

"Yes, definitely." She was pleased he showed excitement about one of her favorite places in Tampa. "And then still not experience all of it."

They strolled through the marketplace stopping for a few minutes here and there to take in outdoor eateries, then stopped and spent thirty minutes observing a cooking class. Around 1:00 PM Carrie's stomach growled.

"You're hungry?"

"I am." Carrie chuckled. Apparently, Kent had heard her gut's cry.

"So am I."

The Florida sunshine gleamed through the vast windows as they sipped sweet tea while contemplating which restaurant to choose.

"So many choices. You pick."

"Steelbach's Chophouse is fabulous." Carrie knew this man would love the steaks that were cooked over a 1000-degree oak fire grille, giving the meat a unique flavor.

"Let's do it."

Kent fell into step beside Carrie as they followed the white concrete sidewalk around to the seating area where the mouth-watering aromas of shrimp vied with those of steak and fries. They were fortunate to find a table with a view of the marina.

Carrie ordered broccoli and cheddar soup followed by shrimp and grits. Today she didn't feel self-conscious when she ate. She felt very comfortable with Kent, and that sent a warm sensation from the top of her head to the tips of her toes.

"Such a vibrant setting," Kent said. "Great food and impeccable service. I am impressed."

"This is a number one attraction for tourists."

"I can see why."

"Stays crowded like this year around."

"And I thought the riverwalk was just a path around the river." He chuckled. "Mom and Dad would be taken with this place."

"My family loves it here."

"I take it you aren't an only child." Kent smiled.

The warm tenor of his deep voice washed over her skin like warm honey. She could listen to him talk all day.

"No. I have two older sisters, Abby and Emily. I'm ten years younger than Emily." She shook her head. "I'm Mom's late-in-life baby."

"I have one younger brother, Carl. He's doing an internship at University of Missouri, Columbia."

"What's his major?"

"He wants to do something in Oncology."

"That would be interesting."

"Our mother is a ten-year stage 4 breast cancer survivor."

Carrie caught the emotion in Kent's voice. She wrapped her arms tightly around her chest and let her gaze linger on him while she waited for him to continue.

"There was a period of time we thought we'd lose her."

"Oh my. That had to be difficult for the entire family."

"It was. When Mom started chemo, we watched her lose her hair, her appetite, and her strength. She was a trooper though. Every step of the way. Even when she barely had enough strength to walk, she kept the faith." Kent's shoulders fell. "It was so hard watching her struggle and fight for her life every day. That's what shifted Carl's interest toward Oncology."

Carrie nodded. "Cancer is a frightening disease."

"It was for us."

"I can't even begin to imagine how I'd feel if Mom or Dad would get cancer." Since her parents had been in their forties when she was born, they were getting on in years. Being in nursing she was aware of the medical problems older adults dealt with.

Kent angled his head, and his pained eyes locked on hers.

"It's not easy watching a parent suffer," he said.

"Does your family live here?"

"No. Carl is engaged to a med student at U of M, so he'll probably make Columbia his home. Mom and Dad will stay in Kansas City."

The waiter passed by with a pitcher of tea and refilled their glasses. "Would you like to see the dessert menu?"

Both shook their heads simultaneously.

"I couldn't hold another bite." Carrie placed a hand on her chest. "Everything was delicious."

After Kent paid for the meal, he took Carrie's arm. "Where now?"

"Oh, we've just begun." She laughed and nudged him toward the pedestrian trail. "Now we walk the 2 ½ miles along the Hillsborough River."

"Good." Kent chuckled. "I need to walk off the calories I just ingested." He entwined her fingers through his.

"That we'll do. I promise."

She couldn't quite describe how his hand in hers made her feel. But she recognized the contentment that flowed over her, pleased with her current situation, not seeking change or improvement. She did not want to release the moment because she hadn't felt this way in a long time.

Carrie enjoyed easy conversation with Kent as they trudged along the trail, stopping to admire the scenery from time to time. At one snack-bar, they even bought a carbonated pineapple slushie, then slid onto a bench and did some people watching.

Two hours later, they headed back to the parking garage.

"I had a blast today." Kent opened the passenger door.

"Me too."

Carrie let him help her scoot into the seat. She gave her handsome escort a sideways glance, enjoying the view. He was so handsome it was hard to take in without losing her breath. Yes, definitely eye candy, she thought.

* * *

Carrie locked the front door after Kent dropped her at her apartment. She leaned her back against the wall, lost in today's emotions. She rehashed their conversations which had made her feel like a wide-eyed, wild-hearted teenager again. Kent had been perfect. Just like Sam and Donnie, she thought. Tenderness for him welled up in her throat and she swallowed hard, recognizing the signs; she was falling for him, fast and hard and she did not want to let him slip away. She couldn't chance losing this man.

After she showered, she grabbed her iPad, plopped down on her bed, then checked her email. Two notes from Emmy and three from Abby. Short messages asking how her day went. Congratulations, etc. Just like her siblings. They didn't want to interrupt her day with a call or text. But they couldn't resist sending the emails.

She started to do a face-time with them when her

cell rang.

"Hey, Kent."

"Hi, beautiful. I'm too wired to sleep."

"Yeah, I know what you mean."

"I wanted to tell you one more time how much I enjoyed today. Everything about it. Especially the company. You made my day, Carrie."

"Yes, it was a good day. I feel the same."

"I would like to see you again."

Carrie's heart danced in her chest. "Same here." She shook her head. Why did she get so tongue tied when she tried to respond to him? He'd opened up. And all she could say is 'same here'. How lame.

"If you're free, how does next Saturday sound?"

"Perfect. I'd love to go out with you again, Kent." Much better, Carrie thought.

"It's a date, then. Good night. Sweet dreams."

"Good night."

Carrie hit end. A warm fuzzy sensation floated over her skin. She laid on top of the covers, basking in the cozy excitement that engulfed her.

CHAPTER SEVEN

After Church on Sunday, Carrie headed to her mom and dad's. The uneventful hour drive to Orlando gave her ample time to contemplate her future. Hopefully with Kent.

"You're the first to arrive," her mom said.

"I'm the only kid ya got that doesn't have anyone but herself to get ready." Carrie tossed her a wink. "At least for now."

"Sounds like everything with your new guy is going well."

"You bet it is."

"Oh, sweetie, I'm so pleased for you."

"Wait until you meet him." Her mind conjured up the handsome face of her new found love. "You are going to adore him."

"I'm very anxious for the introduction."

"Where's Dad?"

"Ball game's started." Her mom shrugged. "He'll join us before long."

Dad, always a big baseball fan, did not want to miss his favorite team. The Tampa Bay Rays were in the playoffs for the World Series. If they made it, Dad would not miss a single game.

"Did I hear my name taken in vain?" Dad stuck his head around the corner, a smile spread from ear to ear.

"Who's winning?" Carrie stepped to her dad's side and let him pull her in for his customary bear hug.

"The Rays are one down."

"They'll catch up." Mom opened the oven and peeked inside.

Carrie ran her hand across a small thick patch of rough, scaly skin on her father's forehead. The center looked a little irritated. "What's this?"

"Just my old dry skin acting up." Dad rolled his eyes.

"Have you had it looked at?"

Carrie figured it was indeed just a dry skin patch. However, she didn't want him to neglect something that could be skin cancer. Thoughts of Kent's mother flashed through her head. She dismissed it. No need to get herself worked up.

"No, he hasn't." Mom shook her head. "He never listens to me."

Carrie saw her father's forehead form wrinkles and he pulled at his chin.

"I know you're worried, Dad."

He couldn't fool her. Carrie understood her dad's

difficulty in articulating his concerns.

"What makes you think I'm worried?"

"Because I know you. You've already built the worst scenario in your mind and don't want to get it confirmed." Carrie blew out a breath. "And that's normal. Don't be afraid to say you're scared."

Dad shook his head. "That's what I get for having a house full of nurses."

"And don't you forget it." Carrie forced a chuckle to cover up her frustration.

"I have my annual check-up next month. I'll have doc look at it then."

"Let me know and I'll meet you there. I want to hear first-hand what the doctor thinks."

"Oh, okay. I'll text you the date."

Noise from the front caught Carrie's ear. She turned and spotted a flurry of family entering the home.

"The gang's here." Abby's voice rang out over the chaotic din.

"Aunt Carrie."

A sweet little niece ran and grabbed Carrie around the legs.

Amanda, too big for Carrie to hoist on her hip anymore, still held up arms to be lifted. Instead, Carrie squatted and hugged the little girl.

"You grow an inch every time I see you." Carrie kissed Amanda's cheek. "You are going to be tall. Just like mommy."

Both of Carrie's sisters were tall and blonde, while she, a complete opposite, was brunette and five-feet-two.

"I go to school now."

"I know you do." Carrie pushed a strand of hair from her niece's forehead. "It's hard to believe you are about to finish first grade."

The rest of the Dennison family marched into the kitchen, filling it with smiles and laughter.

When Adam reached for his aunt, Carrie pulled him into her arms. She could still manage lifting the three-year-old bundle of cuteness.

Carrie studied her sisters and their spouses. Abby and Sam, married six years, still acted like newlyweds. Not gushy and gooey, just affectionate. Carrie often witnessed a subtle look passing between them, or a light touch indicating they'd shared a memory meant only for the two of them.

Emily and Donnie were newlyweds. When she and Donnie admitted, despite past heartbreaks, they belonged together, they didn't delay and had tied the knot ten months ago.

Both of her sisters had experienced rough periods with relationships. Hearts broken and the future looking gloom for them both, they forged on. And now look at them, she thought, they both have their forever loves.

Since meeting Kent, she desired that too. Kent was everything she'd ever wanted. He made her believe she could trust him and let down her defenses, surrender her heart to him. He wouldn't hurt her like Jeff had.

"Earth to Carrie…"

Abby's voice brought Carrie back to the present.

"Sorry, guess I was lost in thought."

"Kent." Abby and Emmy blurted out in unison, then burst into laughter.

All eyes turned to Carrie and she laughed along with her tribe. They knew her so well.

"I'm busted."

* * *

Kent stared at his cell phone. A missed call from Ellen. Oh great. Why would she call him? He thought things had been settled between them before he'd left Kansas City. That's what he got for thinking.

He checked voice mail.

Ellen's voice: "Hey, Kent. Sure do miss you. I'll be in Tampa for a week and will definitely contact you. Looking forward to seeing you. It has been way too long. Hugs."

Ellen was coming to Tampa? Kent rubbed his forehead with two fingers. He could not believe she had the nerve to seek him out. She had tried her best to cause trouble for him in Kansas City, convincing her friends he'd made promises he couldn't keep, then dumped her. Not true, he'd never led her on.

They had met at the hospital, and she'd asked him to join her for dinner and he'd accepted. He liked her well enough, enjoyed her company and they'd had a few dates. But he'd never said the 'L' word. Her feelings for him had escalated to a point she became possessive, wanted his undevoted attention. He couldn't continue a one-sided relationship and tried to let her down as gently as possibly.

When he told her he liked her as a person but was not interested in a romantic commitment, she exploded.

She threatened him.

Fatal Attraction.

While he stared at his phone, it rang, bringing him back to reality.

Ellen.

He let it go to voice mail.

He was not ready to deal with her. Not yet. Soon though. He knew Ellen wouldn't be ignored. She'd pester him until he responded. But he needed time to process this sudden development. He could not fathom what in the world she was trying to prove. She was not an airhead. He would think she'd be smart enough to know you cannot make someone respond to you when they just didn't feel it.

His focus switched to Carrie, complete opposite of Ellen. His feelings for Carrie were complete opposite too. He was attracted to Carrie, and he couldn't deny the chemistry between them. From day one he'd felt a spark ignite and start a forest fire in his soul. When he wasn't with her, he yearned to see her, wanted to hear her voice. More and more his every thought revolved around his encounters with the sweet nurse who'd stolen his heart.

He was falling in love with her.

CHAPTER EIGHT

Kent shaded his eyes from the early evening sun as he surveyed the property surrounding Carrie's apartment complex. Close to Highway 92, and only a short drive to Tampa International Airport. But what he liked best was that she lived not far from his own apartment. Pindo palm trees, single-trunked and erect, lined the driveway. The blue-gray fonds curved toward the trunk, while the petioles had thorns which pointed toward the leaf tip. In between the palms, flowers blossomed. He wasn't sure what they were. Maybe hibiscus? The bright colors erupted with a hint of tropical aroma that permeated the air. Whatever they were, they were attractive and smelled good.

"Are you waiting for me?"

Kent looked down and locked eyes with the

stunning petite woman he'd had on his mind for days. She wore a black and white striped shirt tucked into slim black pants that hugged her curves. Her brunette hair was pushed back with a stylish pair of sunglasses, and her tanned skin looked flawless. Her full lips were punctuated with a light shade of lipstick, making him want to muss it up just a little.

Kent stood there, blinking, as if he'd never seen a beautiful woman before. He was usually much more in control, but something about this woman threw him off his game. He was at a loss for words.

"Well...?" Carrie's laugh pulled him out of his trance.

"Yes, beautiful. I'm waiting for you."

He took her arm and guided her to his jeep, then opened the passenger door. After she slid into the seat, he headed to the driver's side, and scooted under the wheel. Her slender arm situated on the armrest was so close he was blown away by her nearness.

She was even more beautiful close up. Her sweet subtle scent reminded him of the honeysuckle that grew along the fence of his childhood home.

Kent drove to *Ocean Prime* restaurant, located at the entrance to the International Plaza shopping center on the corner of West Shore and Boy Scout Boulevard, an upscale chain known for its sophisticated décor with a classic steak and fresh seafood menu. He'd dined at the one in Kansas City on more than one occasion. Good food. Nice atmosphere.

Last night he'd googled 'nice restaurants in the

Tampa area'. When *Ocean Prime* popped up, he knew where he wanted to take Carrie. He wanted to do something special for his fantastic nurse.

When he pulled into the parking lot, a memory of taking Ellen to the one in Kansas City on their last date washed over him. Only, at the time, he hadn't realized it would be the last date. They'd had a nice dinner and good conversation, or so he thought. Even laughed a lot. The problem happened when he took her home. She insisted he come inside for coffee. When he'd declined, she literally went off on him. Accused him of being a womanizer. She said he'd just toyed with her feelings and used her. Totally shocked, he told her he'd call her the next day, then made a quick exit.

He'd met with her one more time, at a local coffee shop, to break all ties, and it did not go well. But he had not wanted to be alone with her again. He did not want a repeat of the little fit she'd thrown.

He took a deep breath, exhaled the flashback, and grounded himself in the present moment. Taking his focus off of a bad memory minimized its effects on his emotions. Ellen was past. She had never been a serious relationship. And *Ocean Prime* was a good place to take a date. He wasn't going to let his recent voice mail from Ellen ruin the evening.

After Kent guided Carrie inside the restaurant, he stood to her left at the entrance to the dining room and waited for the hostess.

An attractive redhead of about thirty approached. "Good evening. Table for two?"

"Yes, please. Outside if it's available." Kent smiled.

He cupped Carrie's elbow and together they followed the hostess to a table situated under the covered terrace.

Kent waited until Carrie was seated, then he settled in a chair opposite his date. Her beauty and grace continued to amaze him. He'd never felt so mesmerized by a woman before. Just looking at her stirred unfamiliar emotions, making his head spin.

The server brought the menu and a pitcher of ice water. She filled the glasses already placed on the table and Kent thanked her, then opened the menu.

"Good choice." Carrie raised a perfectly plucked eyebrow. "I've not been here before."

"I haven't been to this one. But I've frequented the one in Kansas City several times." Kent picked up his glass. "I hope the food is as good here as it was back home." He took a drink of water to moisten his dry mouth.

"My family is having an informal get-together next weekend." Carrie smiled.

He noticed Carrie's tone had turned the least bit shy. He fell silent and waited for her to continue.

"I'd love for you to come with me. Meet my crazy bunch."

"I'd like that." Kent's spirits kicked up a notch. Wow. Meeting Carrie's family. That's a good sign.

"Great. We're going to meet at Abby's in Platt City."

"Platt City?"

"Takes under 30 minutes to get there. So, if you'd like, you can pick me up at 10 Saturday morning."

"It's a date."

"I hope you like horses."

"If you like them, I can learn to love them." He laughed. That lovely lady made him willing to learn anything it took to please her.

"Abby's husband taught all of us how to ride. We're hooked now."

"I'm game."

Carrie's mouth turned up into a wide grin and she angled her head to the side. That sweet gesture made his heart smile, and he knew, no question about it. He was hooked.

CHAPTER NINE

Monday morning Carrie met her parents at Family Medical Center in Orlando. She wanted to hear first-hand the doctor's opinion.

The waiting room buzzed with hushed chatter as she guided her parents to seats. She signed her dad in at the front desk, then lowered herself onto the padded chair next to her father. The thought of anything threatening the health of her parents, especially cancer, consumed her.

An elderly gentleman seated to her right, hacked into a tissue. His cough rattled, making Carrie suspect an upper respiratory infection. She hoped he wasn't contagious. A young woman with two small children sat across from her. The fussy kids repeated their desire to go home. The young woman ran a hand through her tangled hair while she explained why they couldn't leave just yet.

Carrie tried not to stare at the clients. But unless she angled her head upward and viewed the ceiling, there was nowhere to look except at the people. She stood, crossed to the magazine rack and randomly grabbed a journal published by the local medical clinic. She returned to her seat and instead of checking out her periodical, she made small talk with her dad.

It seemed like hours passed before the nurse called his name. Carrie looked at her watch. Ten-thirty. They'd spent almost an hour in the waiting room. She pulled in a deep breath and tried not to show her irritation when she fell into step behind the nurse who guided her parents through the doorway. Another fifteen minutes slid by before Dr. Sellers entered the exam room.

"Good morning, Mr. Dennison," the doctor said. "I see you have developed an area you're concerned about." His brows pulled together as he looked down at his iPad.

He laid the tablet down and lowered himself onto a stool, then wheeled in front of Dad and eyed his forehead. "When did you first notice this?"

"I don't know. Maybe a few months ago when it first started."

A few months ago? Frustration tied knots in Carrie's gut and she wanted to scream at her father, but she held her tongue. Why hadn't he mentioned this to anyone sooner? Why hadn't she noticed it before?

"A few months?" Dr. Sellers asked. "Two months? Three months? Six months?"

"Probably three months. I've always had problems with dry skin. I figured that's all it was."

"Well, let's take a closer look." The doctor snapped on latex gloves and rolled his stool to the exam table.

Carrie watched while the doctor examined her father's forehead. "This could be early psoriasis," he said. "However, to be on the safe side, I'd like to biopsy the area."

"Now?" Dad asked.

"Yes. I'm going to move you to the procedure room."

Dad groaned.

"It will only take a few minutes, and I will numb the area. You should only feel a little pressure."

"Yeah, I bet." Dad chuckled.

Carrie heard dread in her dad's voice, and she knew her father wished he'd never made this appointment.

When the doc helped him through the doorway, all kinds of thoughts raced through her mind, but she kept them to herself. No need to upset her mother anymore that necessary. She berated herself once again for not paying closer attention to her family. She was a nurse after all. She should have noticed a long time ago.

Tears threatened her eyes by the time the door opened, and Dr. Sellers stepped inside the room.

"I got a good sample." The doctor rubbed his jaw. "And Mr. Dennison did just fine."

"Thank goodness." Carrie released a breath.

Dr. Sellers smiled. "Keep the bandage over the biopsy site until tomorrow. After that, clean the site two times a day. The nurse will be in shortly with written instructions."

"Do you think it's anything to worry about?" A frown crimped Mom's forehead.

The doctor tented his fingers and he met Mom's gaze. "It could be something as simple as eczema or psoriasis. But we'll know for sure when the results come back. I'll get the biopsy sent to the lab and that will show if there are any cancer cells present."

"How soon until we get the results?" Mom asked.

"Shouldn't take too long. Depending on how busy the pathologist is. But I'd guess four or five days at the most."

Mom nodded.

The doctor stood. "The nurse will bring your husband in shortly." He extended his hand toward Mom.

"Thank you." Mom accepted his gesture.

"As soon as the results come in, our office will be in touch with you." Dr. Sellers turned on his heel and headed out the door.

When the nurse escorted Dad into the exam room she explained wound care, then gave Mom everything in written form before she said good day and exited.

"Well, that's that." Dad's eyebrows arched when he glanced between her and Mom. "Now maybe you two can give me a break."

"We love you, Daddy." Carrie threw an arm around her father's waist. "Let us fuss over you."

The smile that spread across her father's face revealed he indeed relished all the fussing his family poured over him.

"I'm springing for lunch," Dad announced firmly.

"Good deal." Carrie laughed.

"You pick," Mom said, and Carrie could hear the gratitude in her voice.

A silent prayer went up for Dad. Carrie prayed for negative biopsy results. Psoriasis, though not the greatest news to hear, sure beat the 'C' word.

"I choose Del Taco." Carrie sing-songed the fast-food logo which made her mom and dad laugh. Funny how hanging with her parents brought out the child in her.

She felt blessed beyond words for loving parents. And she couldn't help worrying about them. Though both still active, she wondered how much longer until the signs of aging raised its ugly head.

Dad golfed with his buddies at least once a month and Mom walked two miles a day, weather permitting. Carrie realized decreased mobility changed a person's lifestyle, and she dreaded the day when her parents were no longer able to maintain their activities of daily living.

"You seem a million miles away." Vertical wrinkles formed between Dad's eyebrows.

"Oh, Dad, I'm right here with you." Carrie ran her tongue across her bottom lip. "More than you could imagine."

They arrived at the fast-food restaurant and ordered tacos and refried beans, which was Carrie's all-time favorite. Then drinks in hand, they sat at a table by the window and watched traffic speed up and down National Drive while they sipped their iced teas.

A young man walked to their table, placed the order in front of them, then hurried away.

"Kent is coming with me to Abby's Saturday." Carrie squeezed hot sauce over her taco.

"Is he an equestrian?" Dad raised a brow.

Carrie laughed. "No, not yet. But I believe he will be. How could he be around the sweet horses at Abby's and not fall in love with them?"

"I agree," Mom said. "Sam made believers out of our entire family."

"I'm anxious to meet this young man you are so hung up on." Dad chuckled.

"Me too." Mom pulled her lunch from the brown bag, unwrapped her taco.

"I am serious about him. I think he could actually be the one." The more time she spent with Kent, the more she realized she could not even think how empty her life would be without him in it. She loved him. *I don't want to do life without him.*

"From what you've told us, he sounds like a keeper." Dad smiled. "I can see how happy you've been lately."

"He does make me happy." Carrie pulled her hair back into a ponytail then let it fall to her shoulders.

Lunch polished off, Carrie rode with her dad to her parked car at the doctor's lot.

"See you Saturday, baby girl." Dad cleared his throat.

Carrie loved that her father still called her his baby girl. Some things never change, Carrie thought. Some things never need to change.

She kissed her mom and dad's cheeks, then

hopped in her car and headed back to Tampa. Back to where she'd left her heart.

CHAPTER TEN

Kent woke at 6 AM, hopped on the treadmill for 30 minutes, showered, grabbed a quick breakfast then headed to work. All in record time. He lived close to public transportation, but he opted to drive the short distance to the hospital even though parking was a challenge. He liked having his vehicle available for unexpected off-site meetings. Also, he could take Carrie to lunch providing both scheduled their lunch breaks at the same time.

At 8 AM he met with his executive secretary. Sheila looked to be in her early twenties. Her very light red hair rested on her shoulders and had a subtle wave to it, an understated wave, so you'd not really be sure if it was a wave at all, or if it was just windblown. She reminded him he had a mentoring meeting with a young executive in the afternoon.

He applauded Sheila's efficient skill. She kept him on track daily.

At 8:30 he attended a Board of Directors' Strategic Planning Committee meeting which covered long-term infrastructure planning and only took forty-five minutes.

After the meeting he made a quick stop in the cafeteria to fill his 16 oz. travel mug with hot coffee, then returned to his office, plopped into his swivel chair, and scooted up to his desk. He entered his PC password and checked e-mails. He sighed when he saw over fifty messages. He prioritized and replied to the key one concerning the purchase of a new MRI machine. If he didn't reply today, he'd not get approval.

Sheila stuck her head around the corner of his office door. "The Vice President for Finance is here, Kent."

"Send him in." Kent shut down his computer and took a long swig of coffee.

The next hour Kent and the VP reviewed preliminary financial results for the prior month. They also scheduled several in-house budget meetings.

"Each department is preparing a proposed budget for the upcoming fiscal year," the VP explained.

"I understand they will have the proposals complete by our next meeting," Kent said. "I talked with several directors last week and they are on schedule."

The VP nodded. "This budget season is especially challenging given some new laws in the state and the competitive landscape in the hospital industry."

"Yes, that's what I understand." Kent massaged his brow and scanned the reports. "I've been looking over the new Florida laws. Quite a challenge."

To Kent's relief, the meeting ended at 10:30, and as soon as the VP headed out, Kent made a bee-line for the breakroom to refill his travel mug again. He had a couple business calls he needed to take care of, and he wanted his caffeine level to remain on an even keel to keep him focused.

When 11:30 rolled around, he made a quick run to the maintenance department to see if the new equipment had arrived. Problems with backorders had been an issue since COVID, and the hospital departments never knew if their supplies would come on time. Fortunately, the Custodial Director reported a large shipment had arrived early this morning.

By noon he craved a Carrie fix, so he boarded the elevator, punched #4 and exited on the Trauma Surgery Unit.

* * *

"Good morning, Mrs. Clayton," Carrie said. "My name is Carrie and I will be your nurse while you are on our unit."

Mrs. Clayton nodded.

Admitted post-surgical hysterectomy, the patient's IV infiltrated and was removed in recovery.

Carrie knew how busy they stayed in the post-anesthesia care unit, and it was no big deal for her to get the IV going again.

After Carrie washed her hands, she used alcohol cleanser, then donned sterile gloves. She made small talk with her client while she checked the vein, cleaned the patient's arm and inserted a needle. The patient flinched, but remained still.

When Carrie saw a flashback of blood in the hub, she knew she was in. She advanced the rest of the cannula into the vein, removed the needle, and applied pressure above the insertion site while she connected the IV tubing. Then she carefully taped the area making sure it was secure.

Mrs. Clayton said, "Thank you. You did a good job. Didn't hurt at all."

"Can you tell me what your pain level is? On a scale of zero to ten. Zero no pain. Ten is the worst pain."

"Probably 3 to 4. Not too bad."

"Okay. I will check on you later." Carrie patted Mrs. Clayton's shoulder.

The patient's half-smile told Carrie sleep would take her under soon.

"If you need anything, press your call button." Carrie handed the apparatus to her patient, explained how to use it, and hoped she would remember.

Carrie stepped to the sink, removed her gloves, then washed her hands.

One last assessment of her new admission satisfied Carrie. She felt assured her patient was comfortable and did not require pain medication at this time.

When she walked to the nursing station, she saw Kent step off the elevator. Three of the floor nurses headed his way, obviously craving his attention. But when he saw her, he sidestepped the nurses and headed toward Carrie.

"Hey, beautiful," Kent said.

He kept his voice low, and Carrie had to strain to hear him.

Carrie grinned when she noticed the expression on her three co-workers' faces. They were so envious of her. She smiled. *I would be, too.*

"Any chance you can take your lunch break?"

"As fate would have it, I just finished with my last morning patient."

"What luck."

His eyes crinkled and his full sensuous upturned lips seemed to beg for a kiss. She felt her stomach do somersaults.

"Give me a minute to check out."

When she turned to walk away, she could practically feel the heat of his stare warming her skin. Her pulse raced, and heat rushed to her cheeks.

What was it about this CEO that made her feel like a teenager in love?

CHAPTER ELEVEN

Carrie headed to the salad bar in the cafeteria. She filled her tray with a grilled chicken salad, ranch dressing on the side and a large, iced tea. After finding an empty table, she took a seat and watched Kent breeze through the hub-bub, tray filled with delectables, then head her way. He sat in the chair opposite her.

"Ummm. That looks good." Carrie eyed Kent's Quiche Lorraine. The roasted mini potatoes on the side appeared to be crispy, and she resisted the urge to fork one and pop it in her mouth.

"Take a bite."

Kent met her gaze and she wondered if he'd read her mind.

Carrie threw her reserve aside and forked a crispy potato.

"I like a woman who isn't shy about eating with her guy."

Her guy. Yes, he was her guy. She tossed him a wink then held up her fork and looked at the morsel before slipping it into her mouth.

"Has your morning been as busy as mine?" Kent stabbed his fork into the quiche and cut off a hunk.

"Not too bad. Just the usual. A couple admissions, but they went smooth."

Kent nodded while he chewed.

"What's on your schedule for this afternoon?" Carrie asked him.

"First thing I'm going to meet with the Chief Operating Officer and the Chief Nursing Officer to discuss plans to expand outpatient services."

"That's great." Carrie smiled. Outpatient services had been an issue at Tampa General for decades. She was happy to have a CEO who cared, not only about the executive side of a hospital, but also about the nursing aspect. "We've needed that for a long time."

Kent nodded. "Yes, I picked up on that from day one."

Carrie pulled the wrapper off her straw, inserted it into her tea. Ed had been a wonderful CEO, but the last year, with retirement on his mind, he tended to let ideas for updated innovations slide. She guessed he believed a new and younger replacement would be on the ball and get things up to date. One who had a vision for excellent patient care.

"I'm looking forward to meeting your family on Saturday, Carrie."

"They can't wait to meet you, too."

Carrie watched Kent while he forked a small crispy potato, then held it toward her. She smiled and accepted the bite.

"I'm going to warn you, I'm a city boy. I've never been around horses and have no idea how I'd feel about riding."

Carrie laughed. "That's exactly how Abby felt when she first met Sam."

"So I'm not the only greenhorn?"

"Nope."

"That's a relief. I don't want to come across to your family as a sissy."

"Never." She pressed her lips together. "I doubt anyone would ever mistake you for a sissy."

"Good."

"I'm sure Sam would be happy to meet with you one on one and give you some great pointers. Abby knew nothing about riding when she met Sam."

"Cool."

"And believe me, Abby's an expert now."

"Sounds like your entire family excels at riding."

"Thanks to Sam."

"You've never mentioned, what does your brother-in-law do?"

Carrie could not help herself, she burst into a full-blown fit of laughter.

"What?"

Carrie regained her composure, smoothed down her collar. "Just wait until you hear this story."

Kent cocked his head to the side. "I'm ready."

A few minutes later, after Carrie had told him the saga about Sam and Abby, she swallowed down the last of her tea.

"No kidding. He's a physician?"

"Yep."

"Pretended to be a janitor?"

Carrie nodded. "I couldn't make something that outlandish up."

"Sounds like you're taking the story of their life straight from a romance novel."

"Well, my sister was destined to love again, and she found her forever love." Maybe just like her, she thought. But she stayed silent. Eating off his fork made her feel like they'd made a step forward in intimacy, but she didn't feel this was the time nor the place to declare her love for him.

"I can't wait to meet them." Kent arched a brow. "Is there a story about your other sister?"

Carrie chuckled.

"Oh my. Fill me in."

"Emily married a full-fledged drug addict."

"Nah."

"He's clean now. Has been for some time. He's an accountant."

"That's a relief."

"Emily has an interesting history. I'll share details with you some other time."

"Okay," Kent said.

He tossed her a puzzled look.

"But things are good in her life now."

Kent nodded.

"She also found her forever love."

"Well, that's the important thing. And I can wait for the details until you're ready to share."

"It's a long story." Carrie looked up at the huge wall clock in the cafeteria. "And we're running out of time."

"No problem. We'll talk again. I want to learn everything about you and your family."

Carrie loved how compassionate this man could be. Kent's steady gaze enveloped her and said more than mere words could express, making her heart fill with hope.

* * *

After lunch when Kent returned to his office, Carrie's clean, fresh scent lingered. Why was there a weird fluttery feeling in his chest whenever he thought of his nurse? He smiled and answered his question. Because she's smart, beautiful, and a little sassy. She'd blown into his life like a windstorm, and from that day forward, she'd turned his life upside down.

When she'd talked about her sisters finding their forever love, he'd hoped she would consider him her happy ending. He knew he wanted her to be his forever after.

He scooted up to his desk and glanced over his afternoon's schedule. Time to meet with the architects to review his plans for a new ambulatory surgery suite which would improve patient care. He'd worked on the plan since he'd first toured Tampa General.

He gathered his information and headed to the conference room. Introductions were shared, and he learned Jim and Walter were the architects.

"What exactly are you proposing?" Walter asked.

"I would like to create a 23,000-square-foot facility which would feature state-of-the-art operating rooms, recovery areas, and a pre-surgical testing suite."

"That's double the current size," the other gentlemen told him.

The first architect scribbled numbers on the notepad in front of him.

"Yes. I am aware of that. I'm excited that we would be able to provide quality care for our patients." Kent jotted a note on his pad to discuss the new facility with the public relations department.

The architects took a few minutes, looked through the proposal, scribbled some more numbers, then quoted a preliminary cost for the expansion.

"That is doable." Kent ran a hand through his hair. He was pleased that the quote fell within his anticipated cost. He could already picture the new addition.

"We will have the final dollar amount on your desk early next week."

"Great," Kent said. "I'll meet with the board and, if everything's a go, I will let you know when the project can begin." Kent rubbed his chin. "We're always looking for an edge in this competitive market, and this is a great way to educate the public about our services and facilities."

The architects stood and tucked their notes into their briefcases.

"Thank you for your input, and I look forward to hearing from you soon." Kent watched the gentlemen gather the blueprints.

Pleased with the outcome of the meeting, and after a few cordial pleasantries, Kent walked with them to the door, then watched them disappear down the hall. He pulled in a relieved breath. He could see great things happening at Tampa General. With the hospital. With Carrie.

Kent laid his notes on his desk, then headed to the cafeteria to meet with a young executive over coffee to discuss career interests and goals. He intended to strongly encourage her to get more involved with professional associations in the industry. Such an excellent way to raise her profile, learn new skills through continuing education, and help others via volunteering.

What he hadn't counted on, was her invitation to dinner.

Of course he declined.

CHAPTER TWELVE

Saturday turned to rain.

Just as well, Kent thought when he walked Carrie to the front door of her sister's house. Now no excuses needed for delaying his horseback riding inexperience.

"Are you ready to meet my rowdy bunch?" Carrie tossed him a lopsided grin.

"You betcha." He was more than ready to, not only meet, but get to know her family.

Noise from the belly of the house got his attention when Carrie took his hand and led him through the entranceway.

Two tall blondes walked quickly toward them.

"Kent," Carrie said. "I would like you to meet my two sisters." She motioned to the one on the right. "This is Abby."

"So happy to meet you, Abby."

"And this is Emmy. Emily." Carrie motioned toward the one on the left.

"Very nice to meet you, too."

Neither of the sisters looked the least bit like Carrie.

"I hear you're the new CEO at Tampa General." Abby shifted from one foot to the other. "How do you like it?"

"I like it. Happy I took the position and relocated."

"Obviously, I'm happy too," Carrie said. "Otherwise, I would have met my waterloo with a big black dog."

"I'm sure you would have pulled through somehow." Kent smiled.

He would never forget the fateful day that changed his life.

"Come on in and meet the rest of the gang." Emily walked through a doorway and motioned him to follow.

Carrie cleared her throat. "Mom, Dad, this is Kent Acuff."

"Nice to meet you, Mr. and Mrs. Dennison."

"I don't want to hear any of that Mr. and Mrs." Carrie's father shook his head briskly. "I'm Ted. This is Sally."

"Okay, then it's Ted and Sally."

Kent lost track of names for a minute while Carrie introduced him to the rest of her clan. He hoped he'd get the names down pat before the end of the day.

"Come in the den." Sam nodded toward a

doorway across the room. "It's too noisy in here to hear ourselves think, much less get acquainted."

Kent followed Sam and Donnie into a spacious living area.

"Very nice." Kent scanned the room.

"Officially it's my man cave, but I have to admit, Abby spends a lot of time in here with me. If there's a movie we want to catch, we always watch it in here."

Kent eyed the strategically placed couches and ottomans placed in front of what he guessed to be a custom built-in entertainment center. The couches looked perfect for relaxing, watching sports, and everything in between."

"That's got to be the largest flat screen TV available." Kent chuckled.

Sam nodded. "It's 98 inches. Great for ballgames. You feel like you are sitting in the stadium."

"Next best thing to sitting in the stadium," Donnie said. "Emily and I head over here to catch the Rays on their night games."

Sam nodded and his eyebrow lifted. "You and Carrie need to join us for their next game."

"That sounds good."

Kent, a Kansas City fan, rooted for KCs baseball and football teams. But since he now resided in Tampa, he'd add the Rays and Buccaneers to his list.

"Can I get you guys anything to drink?" Sam asked.

Kent watched Sam head to built-in cabinetry faced in brass diamond-patterned grilles. An apartment sized refrigerator housed in the cabinet, with a small sink underneath and hotplate on top, looked perfect for entertaining.

"Name your poison. I've got bottled water, coke, diet coke, sprite and Gold Peak sweet and sugar free tea."

"I'll take a bottled water." Donnie rubbed his chin.

"Sweet tea for me." Kent liked the brand of tea Sam offered.

He watched Sam retrieve two bottled waters and a tea, then walk to a circular table with four chairs pushed neatly under the edge. He set the drinks down and said, "Grab a drink, and let's get comfortable."

Kent picked up the tea, removed the cap and took a drink.

"I thought we could get to know each other while the gals whip up some food." Sam motioned to a recliner and said to Kent, "Take the seat of honor."

"Yeah, right." Donnie sat down on the oversized sofa. "Don't let him kid you. He has his place marked."

Sam crinkled his nose, then plopped down in the second recliner, reached to the side, pulled a lever and rode the chair into a reclining position."

Kent laughed. He liked these two guys. Carrie's description was correct, they both seemed easy to know. Easy to like.

"So you're a CEO." Sam rubbed his chin. "I hope it's going well for you. That is a big responsibility to take on."

Kent nodded. "So far, things seem to be going

smooth. I've presented a few new ideas to the Board of Directors. They seem receptive to up-to-date suggestions. They told me they will back my projects providing I don't go over budget."

"That's great." Sam released the lever and sat erect in his recliner. "I worked in a hospital in Atlanta for several years. Oncology. The Board of Directors at that hospital were very rigid. Gave our CEO a run for his money."

"That's too bad." Kent shook his head. He knew how difficult it was to work with someone who closed off to any suggestion presented.

"I'm happy to hear your Board doesn't seem to be like that."

"So far I haven't had any problems with them."

"I'm relieved I don't have to deal with a Board of Directors," Donnie chimed in. "The only one I answer to is sweet Margaret who is the CEO of her small firm. She's a keeper."

"Donnie doesn't have any problems because he's a top-notch accountant. And he never gets any complaints," Sam said.

Donnie shook his head. "I think you might be exaggerating."

"I'll know who to come to when it's tax time." Kent changed position, then crossed his legs.

"I guarantee you will definitely get a discount." Donnie smiled.

"Thanks."

"What made you leave oncology, Sam?" Kent rubbed the back of his neck.

"I worked in pediatric oncology and became very close to my last patient and her family. When she died, I felt I'd lost my own child." Sam stood, walked to the fridge and retrieved three more drinks. "To make a long story short, seeing the kids die on my watch finally got to me."

Kent understood the sadness he saw reflected in Sam's eyes.

"My brother, Carl, is interested in oncology," Kent said. "He's doing his Internship in Columbia, Missouri."

"It's a great field to pursue." Sam passed out the drinks. "More physicians are needed in that specialty. Cancer seems to be on the rise."

"Yeah." Donnie ran a hand through his unruly hair. "I've noticed that."

"Mom is a stage 4 breast cancer survivor. She's fine now, but we nearly lost her." Kent cleared his throat. He could see compassion in both men's faces. "When Carl witnessed first-hand what Mom and our family went through, he decided he wanted to intervene and maybe save lives."

"I get that," Sam said. "My final decision to leave Atlanta came when I landed a job as a custodian at my estranged daughter's boarding school. I wanted to be near her and get a chance to bond with her." Sam's eyes narrowed. "Best move I've ever made. Not only did I bond with Sara, I met Abby."

"When did you open your private practice?"

"After Abby and I got married and Sara and I were on good terms, I decided I couldn't just toss my education aside. I love being a doctor. I just chose the wrong field, for myself that is."

"Good choice," Donnie said. "And the best

decision. One that you can live with."

Kent said, "I'm pleased things worked out for you. Carrie tells me your clinic is doing so well you've hired a Nurse Practitioner."

"Yes. The NP is a big asset to me."

The door sliding open caught Kent's attention. He smiled when he saw Carrie step through the doorway.

"Okay you guys, it's time to eat," she said.

CHAPTER THIRTEEN

"**H**ope you're hungry." Carrie laid her hand on Kent's elbow, nudging him toward the kitchen. "Abby's fixed enough to feed all of Platt City."

Carrie smiled, aware her brothers-in-law had taken Kent under their wing, friended him and made him feel at ease. Guys needed guy friends. Just like girls needed girl time.

Carrie took her CEO's hand when all the gang were seated, and Abby asked Sam to bless the food.

Sam prayed. "Lord, we thank you for family and friends gathered here today, and we ask that you watch over each one of us. Bless this food to our bodies and bless the hands that prepared it. Amen."

Amens echoed around the room.

Carrie took a chicken leg from the platter, then passed the dish to Kent.

She watched Kent take a thigh. He likes the dark meat, Carrie thought. One more thing we have in common.

"Mama, I want the one with the handle too," Samantha said.

Carrie forked the other leg and laid it on baby girl's plate.

"We like the handles, don't we, Aunt Boo Boo?"

"We sure do, sweetie."

When the potatoes were passed, Carrie served herself and her niece.

"It's still raining." Donnie nodded toward the window. "Doesn't look like we'll get to ride today."

"I'm disappointed, too." Sam pulled his brows together.

Carrie knew Donnie loved horseback riding. From what Abby had shared with her, Donnie and Emily looked forward to afternoons on Sam's trail. That usually happened every get together, weather permitting. Unfortunately, today would not be one of those days. However, she sensed her handsome CEO felt relieved. He'd described himself as a 'city boy'. When Sam finished Kent's training, she imagined he'd be as hooked on the horses as the rest of the family.

"We can't control the weather," Donnie said. "We'll have another day to ride."

"Always another day." Carrie glanced at Kent and lowered her voice. "You lucked out, didn't you?"

"Big time." Kent smiled and leaned toward her. "Sam invited me out for a one on one so I can get acquainted with the horses without a crowd."

"Sam's a sweetheart."

"No whispering," Abby said and laughed. "No secrets between the Dennison sisters."

"Since when?" Emily scooted her chair back from the table. "We were born to keep secrets."

"Not!" Carrie laced her fingers together. "We couldn't keep a secret from each other if we tried. Not even if we were paid big bucks."

"Ya think?" Emily's voice turned serious.

"At least not for very long." Abby laughed.

Carrie bit down on her lower lip when she remembered the secret she'd kept all this time. How she had begged Jeff to take her back. Why had she let herself become so dependent on him? Well, that was in the past. She wouldn't dwell on it.

Emily picked up a glass, held it in the air, and gently tapped the side with a butter knife. "Speaking of secrets, Donnie and I have something we want to share with all of you."

"What have you been keeping from us?" Abby laughed.

"Yeah, out with it." Carrie sat straighter in her chair, all ears for the confession.

"Well. . ." Emmy paused, reached for her husband's hand.

Donnie leaned a little closer to his wife, and Carrie could see the love flowing between them.

Emmy continued. "Donnie and I contacted a surrogacy agency."

"When?" Abby's eyes grew round.

"A few months back."

"What?" Carrie pulled in a calming breath. "And you never told us?"

"We wanted to check things out before we said anything. We didn't know how we'd react once we learned all the details."

Carrie was stunned. "So, fill us in."

Emmy nodded. "After we checked out several different agencies, we picked the one in Tampa Bay, which seemed to have the best security system in place to protect all involved."

Carrie looked around the table. Everyone remained quiet, waiting on Emily to continue.

"After we filled out an application, we were called in for a lengthy interview."

"What if the surrogate mother changes her mind after the baby is born?" Mom twisted her napkin around her finger. "I've heard heartbreaking stories."

Emily shrugged. "Yes, there can be bad outcomes if you don't go through a reputable agency."

"I assume you both have done the research," Abby said.

"Extensive." Emily laughed.

"And we found Tampa Bay is very thorough," Donnie said.

Emily nodded. "They propose a match based on the criteria provided by the surrogate and the intended parents."

"The psychological evaluation is extensive, covering every aspect of the surrogate's personal history and background," Donnie said. "Then Emmy and I and the potential surrogate had to have a complete physical."

"The agency hooked us up with an attorney who

will take care of all the legal cases. He specializes in surrogacy issues," Emily said. "The gestational surrogate has no genetic ties to the child because it isn't her egg that is used. There is no way she could ever change her mind and ask for visitation or custody."

"I thought the surrogate provided her own egg. Is that not true?" Dad asked.

"Some people still go that route, but using an egg donor is the safest way to go."

Dad nodded. "I see."

Though he'd said he understood, Carrie could see the confusion in Dad's eyes. Apparently so did Emmy judging by the look on her face.

"Dad, the agency obtains an egg from a donor known only to the agency. The surrogate has no idea who it is. And the egg doner has no idea who her egg will go to. The sperm will be from Donnie," Emily said and squeezed his hand. "Our child will be from Donnie's loins. His flesh and blood. Who could not love a baby like that?"

Everyone laughed. Even Dad.

"Once parenthood is established, the surrogate has no legal rights to the child and she cannot claim to be the mother. Because technically she is not. And since we are not using the surrogate's egg, the process will take time. Could take up to two years. But we don't care. We are willing to take the extra time."

"This is not cheap, but Emily and I have talked it over extensively and we both agree, the cost will be worth it."

"This is so exciting!" Carrie jumped to her feet,

threw arms around the necks of her sister and brother-in-law. "I am so happy for you guys."

The rest of the family gathered around Emily, offering congratulations, crying, laughing, and all the things the Dennison family did to celebrate the happiness of one of their clan.

Carrie noticed when tears surfaced in Emily's eyes and spilled over and her elated sister gushed, "I'm gonna be a mother. I never thought it could be possible. But I'm gonna have a baby!"

Carrie scooted back into her seat and nibbled on a celery stick. Her eyes focused on Kent. "I told you we were a crazy bunch."

"Crazy wonderful." He met her gaze and his face lit up. "Your family is the best."

After helping Abby with the dishes, Carrie and Kent held rain jackets over their heads then darted to the stable for a look at the horses.

"Can you smell it?" The aroma of the stable made Carrie feel all cozy and warm.

He nodded. "I can."

Carrie sucked in a breath when he leaned toward her, then draped one arm around her waist. She slowly blew out her suspended breath and tried to regain equilibrium. When he cupped her chin with his strong palm, she felt dizzy. His face was inches from hers, and his nearness overwhelmed her. The aroma of horses and his woodsy scent with a hint of lime wafted over her and made her knees quiver.

She closed her eyes when she felt gentle lips take hers. His kiss was soft, ever so warm, and she never wanted his mouth to leave hers. His arms circled her, and he pulled her close while she lifted her arms then slid them around his neck. The kiss grew stronger and his four o'clock shadow tickled her cheek leaving her breathless. After several seconds, he stepped back, and she saw passion in his eyes. She felt certain her eyes told the same story.

"We better get back." Kent cleared his throat. His voice was husky, only a step above a whisper with the slightest tremble.

She nodded. She dared not speak.

Walking hand in hand back to the house, the heavy drizzle continued, but they didn't bother to cover their heads, just let the raindrops splatter them. Carrie realized they had made a huge step in their relationship. No going back. Not for her. She was too far in to ever walk away now. She loved him. Loved everything about him.

Emmy's eyes grew round when she opened the door. "I wondered if you guys got lost." She handed each of them a towel.

"Got carried away admiring the steeds." Carrie dabbed at her hair with the towel.

Emily leaned close and whispered, "Yeah, I bet that's what you got carried away doing."

Heat flooding her cheeks, Carrie swatted her sister on the forearm.

CHAPTER FOURTEEN

Kent's lips still felt the warmth and sting of his nurse's mouth long after he'd pulled away. He'd wanted to kiss her for some time but didn't want to rush it and scare her off. Today in the stable, he could not wait one more minute to give her a real kiss and feel her snuggled in his arms. He relished every second he'd held her. It felt so good, so right, and he knew she was the one. He'd come close to declaring his love to her but held back. As bad as he wanted to rush things along and go full speed ahead, he did not want to come on too strong and frighten her away.

He watched her towel drying the raindrops from her silky brunette locks and her movement made him catch his breath. He tried to swallow, but his mouth suddenly went dry. He knew he was busted when she turned and caught him staring at her.

"Sorry," he said. "I can't help myself."

"It's okay," Carrie met his gaze. "I like looking at you, too."

* * *

Later that evening after Kent dropped Carrie at her apartment, he drove home, showered, shaved, then slipped into PJ bottoms and curled up in his recliner. He couldn't remember feeling this contented with life. His job was good. He'd made several new friends. But best of all, he'd found Carrie. On that all-important day in the park, when he'd seen her plop hard on the ground, little did he think for one minute he'd fall in love with her. But he had. He could admit it now. He loved Carrie Dennison.

He turned on the TV and flipped through channels, but couldn't find anything that interested him, so he settled for the news. He hadn't heard the latest report today. He had nearly dozed off when his phone vibrated, jarring him out of his half-drugged state.

He didn't look at the ID, just said, "Hello."

Big mistake.

"Well, hello Kent," Ellen said. "I've been trying to get hold of you for several days."

"Oh yeah."

"Yeah. Are you trying to avoid me or something?"

"I've been busy."

"Too busy for me. . .?"

"Ellen, what are you trying to prove? You know we ended this months ago. Now all of a sudden you contact me."

"I never ended anything. It was you. All you."

"I explained everything to you when we ended it."

"So sue me. I didn't buy it for one minute. I knew you loved me. You just ended it because you planned to move to Tampa and didn't think I would go with you. But you were wrong, Kent. I'd follow you anywhere. I'm here now. I plan to stay here. For you. For me and you."

Cold fingers raced up Kent's spine. What in the world was wrong with that woman? She lived in a fantasy world. All make believe. How could she possibly believe he loved her? He had never even hinted that he wanted more than a friendship. Yes, they'd dated. How many times? Four? Five at the most. He'd never wanted to take the relationship farther than a friendship, but she wasn't having it. Her possessive and demanding personality made him sorry he'd ever friended her.

"What do you say. Are you ready to give us another shot?"

"Absolutely not. Ellen, you know as well as I do there never was an us. It was all in your head. "

"Why?"

"What do you mean, why?"

"Why did you ask me out in the first place if you weren't interested in me?"

"If you recall, you asked me out."

"I did not."

"We were at the conference table after a meeting.

You looked at me and said, and I quote, 'I'm going to grab a bite to eat at Joe's BBQ. Want to join me?"

"Whatever."

"Ellen, please can't you drop this? Just let it go, for Pete's sake."

"You're too stubborn to admit how you feel about me."

"Stop it. I'm done. I'm going to hang up now. There isn't any rational way to reach you. You refuse to listen to reason."

"Don't you dare hang up on me," Ellen screamed.

Her voice vibrated in Kent's ear, and he held the phone away from his face. He didn't need her drama. Not now. Not ever.

"Goodbye, Ellen. Please do not call me again." He hit end and rubbed his temple with two fingers. He did not believe for a second this would be the last he heard from the deranged woman.

After Ellen, he was in no mood to watch the news. It was way too depressing, so he flipped the TV off and headed to the bedroom. He picked up his cell.

And hit Carrie's memory button.

* * *

Carrie's phone buzzed and Kent's smiling face exploded across the screen.

"Hey, Kent."

"Hi, beautiful. Just wanted to hear your voice one more time before I call it a night."

"Is everything okay?" She thought she heard a hint of distress in his tone.

"It is now, beautiful. The sound of your voice makes my world rock."

Carrie ran her tongue across her lower lip. "You sure know how to make a girl feel special."

"You are special."

Carrie felt a momentary hitch in her chest at the obvious love and affection in his voice. He always made her heart do leaps under her ribcage.

CHAPTER FIFTEEN

Carrie inhaled the sweet scent of fresh-cut-flowers when she walked through the doorway of her sister's boutique. She scanned the shop Emily and her best friend, Holly, both nurses, opened because they'd grown weary with the medical drama. Her sister's success in the florist business filled Carrie with pride.

"Hey, Boo Boo," Emily said.

"Are you going to close the shop today or not?" Carrie stepped to the counter and tossed her sister a faux frown.

"I wondered if you'd remember our night out since you've found Mr. Hunk of All Time." Emily chuckled.

"Never. Once a month, come rain or shine, the Dennison sisters meet." Carrie pulled her cell from her purse and aimed it toward her sister. "Abby is going to meet us at the restaurant. I just need to text her where we're going tonight."

"Your turn to pick."

"I'm craving pizza, if that's okay with you."

"Fine with me."

"Pizza Hut, on National?"

"Sounds perfect," Abby said. "I'll wash my hands and run a comb through my hair."

Carrie nodded while she texted the info to Abby.

A few minutes later, both sisters pushed through the front doorway of the boutique, and Carrie watched while Emmy locked the door, then pull on the handle to make sure it fastened.

Carrie rode with her sister a few miles through mild traffic, and less than ten minutes later, Emmy found a place to park at their destination.

When Abby pulled in beside them, they slid out of the car and the three sisters, arm in arm, walked through Pizza Hut's doorway. The aroma of tomato sauce and oregano made Carrie's stomach growl. She loved pizza and could eat it every day. They picked a rear booth by a window overlooking North National Avenue. Indirect light brightened the spot, and Carrie blinked away the brightness of the fast-setting sun.

The waiter ambled over. He smiled and aimed a pen at his note pad. "Buffet?"

"Yes," Abby said. "And three sweet teas."

Carrie smiled at her oldest siblings take-charge persona. For some reason when the three sisters were together, they seemed to fall into the age status. Oldest, middle child, baby of the family.

Strange how easy it was to fall back into childhood roles. However, it always made Carrie feel safe and loved.

They headed to the buffet, and minutes later, juggling plates piled high with pizza and salad, they settled into the booth.

"Any big plans for the weekend?" Emily slid her straw into the glass of tea.

"Nothing big," Abby said and laughed. "Sam's scheduled a check-up for the horses Saturday afternoon."

"Time for that already?" Carrie asked. She knew Sam was particular with his horses and kept their hooves trimmed and shaped, and re-shod as needed.

"Yes." Abby picked up a cheese stick. "And Sam plans to invite Kent to come out that morning for his first riding lesson, and let him get used to being around the horses."

"Good." Carrie shook a heavy dose of parmesan on her pizza. "I know he'll love riding once he gets the hang of it."

"And you'll love having yet one more thing in common with him." Emmy's face lit up.

Carrie grinned. "You're right." Seemed like more and more commonalities developed between her and the handsome CEO every day.

"Holly is having a huge sale." Emily's face formed a frown. "And my gullible husband got snookered into helping his big sister. Believe me, I'm not looking forward to that."

"Is she moving?" Abby asked.

"No. She's just got junk everywhere. So, she's having an auction."

Carrie shook her head. "That sounds like a lot of work."

"Uh huh," Emmy said. "And she thinks it'll be fun. She's my best friend, but I tell you, sometimes she is weird."

Carrie laughed and picked up a slice of steaming pepperoni pizza. She sank her teeth into the wedge and the first bite burst with flavor, hot, salty, and spicy. She chewed and swallowed. "I don't have any plans. Just hang out with my guy."

"It's good to see you so happy." Abby picked up her glass.

Not to be left out, Emmy said, "Kent is just what the doctor ordered. He's put spunk back in your personality."

Carrie smiled. She felt her sister's support.

"You guys can't imagine how much I've dreamed about being this happy."

"Oh yes, we can." Her two siblings chimed in at the same time.

The server stepped up to the table and eyed the drinks. "Refill?"

They nodded.

"Back in a jiff."

He scooped up three glasses in one swift movement, a feat Carrie knew she'd never be coordinated enough to manage. Not without a disaster.

"Mom adopted a puppy." Carrie forked some salad and popped it in her mouth.

"From the shelter?"

"No." Carrie shook her head. "Someone dumped him off. And you know Mom, she couldn't call animal control."

"I don't blame her. Those places are wrong." Emmy frowned and dabbed her mouth with a napkin. "He's lucky he was dumped on Mom's street."

"Right. He looks healthy, so I hope he hasn't been mistreated." Carrie tucked a strand of hair behind her ear.

"What kind is he?" Emmy asked.

"Just a mutt. But he's adorable. Black with a white ring around one eye."

"Does she plan to keep him or find him a forever home?" Emmy asked.

Carrie shrugged. "She says find him another home."

"We'll see." Abby's mouth turned up at the corners.

"I'm betting she won't part with him." Carrie shook her head. "You know how Mom loves animals."

Light banter about the puppy continued, but eventually the conversation drifted to Carrie's favorite discussion, her relationship with Kent. Just talking about him and the connection they'd quickly formed made Carrie feel warm and cozy. She hadn't felt like this in a long time. Much too long.

"You hit the jackpot with Kent." Abby raised a brow. "He's definitely good for you."

"I second that." Emmy stifled a yawn and looked at her watch. "Yikes, it's after 10."

"I'm ready to call it a night." Carrie pushed her plate aside. Suddenly she wanted to see Kent or at least hear his voice. She smiled, recognizing the sudden heat that rushed to her cheeks whenever she thought about him.

"I'm stuffed," Abby said. "I bet I've gained five pounds."

"Yeah, right. You know you never gain an ounce no matter how much you eat. I'm the one that's going to pay for this." Emily's face formed frown lines, and she pointed to her two empty plates on the table. "Why did you guys let me eat so much?"

Carrie laughed. "As health professionals, you'd think we would know better." She scooted back from the table, grabbed the ticket, and stood. "My treat this time. See you guys later."

CHAPTER SIXTEEN

Saturday Kent pulled his jeep into Sam and Abby's driveway at 8 AM.

Sam met him at the front door, dressed in blue jeans, a polo shirt and Lacers.

"Ready for your first lesson?" Sam asked.

"As ready as I'll ever be." Kent laughed, trying to disguise his nervousness. He wanted to fit in with Carrie's family, and if horseback riding pleased her, he was more than willing to give it a try.

"Okay." Sam motioned him inside. "First let's get a bite to eat. Kids have already had their breakfast. Now Abby's making ham and cheese omelets for us."

"Sounds good."

Kent hadn't realized how hungry he was until the scent of eggs simmering in butter hit him full force.

He stepped into the kitchen and Abby gave him a wide smile.

"Carrie told me ham and cheese was your favorite," Abby said. "So have a seat, it'll be done in a couple minutes."

Kent felt a ping of delight ricochet off his heart. Carrie not only remembered what he liked, she'd shared it with her sister. He pulled out a kitchen chair and slid into the seat across from Sam. He watched Abby finishing the omelets. She resembled Emily but neither of them looked like Carrie. All three sisters were beautiful. However, he preferred the petite brunette.

Kent glanced to the right just in time to see a young lady step into sight. She led Samantha by the hand and carried Adam on her hip. Her gaze met his and she gave him a timid smile.

"Kent, you've met two of my kiddos." Sam stood. "Now I want you to meet my oldest daughter, Sara."

"Nice to meet you, Sara." Ken stood, extended his hand.

"Nice to finally meet you, too." Sara accepted his greeting.

"He's Boo Boo's hunk." Samantha danced in a circle, clapping her hands.

"Samantha!" Abby's cheeks turned deep red. "You shouldn't blurt out things like that."

Kent smiled when Samantha leaned forward and spoke in a confidential whisper. "It's what Sara called him, Mama."

The child then turned and flashed a brilliant smile while she gazed up at him through long thick lashes.

Sara's nose wrinkled. "I am so sorry." She tugged Samantha's hand, then adjusted Adam on her hip.

"Don't be." Kent laughed. "I've been called worse."

"I've told you to be careful what you say if front of your little sister." Abby's eyes narrowed.

Kent noticed though Abby sounded firm, she looked as though she were trying to repress a laugh.

"Let me down." Adam squirmed, and Kent watched while Sara placed her little brother's feet on the floor.

Adam raced across the room like a stock car.

"Sara's spending the weekend with us," Sam said. "She's in her junior year at University of Florida." Sam's mouth turned up in a smile that revealed how proud he was of his oldest daughter.

Kent gave Sara a thumbs up. "What are your plans after you graduate?"

Sara shrugged. "I want to get my masters, be a Nurse Practitioner."

"That's a good field to enter." Kent knew more and more physicians were relying on the NPs.

When Samantha wandered up to Kent and looked him in the eye, he smiled.

"Where is my aunt Boo Boo?"

"I guess you've figured out Carrie's nickname is Boo Boo," Abby explained. "Not that she likes it."

"I gathered as much." Kent hoisted the little girl up on his knee. "Boo Boo is at work. She doesn't get every Saturday off."

"You're the big boss. Let her off."

"Enough is enough, little gal." Abby walked to the table and pulled Samantha from his lap. "Go play with your dolls for a while my sweet little inquisitive one."

Samantha scampered across the floor. "Quisitive me. Quisitive me."

Abby shook her head. "That girl."

"Both your children are adorable. Don't let Samantha's impromptu outburst fluster you. Be thankful she's so observant."

"Oh, that she is." Sam shook his head. "Sometimes she thinks she's grown."

Kent patted Adam on the head when Sara walked by with the toddler in tow. It was obvious she adored her siblings.

"So nice to meet you, Kent." Sara hoisted Adam on her hip and followed Samantha out of the kitchen. "Don't be a stranger."

Kent nodded. Being a frequent visitor was certainly part of his agenda.

After the omelet and two cups of coffee, Kent trailed Sam to the stable. The aroma of hay and horses blending together wafted over him, reminding him of Carrie. And the kiss. He had to admit he enjoyed the scent.

"That's Hero." Sam pointed toward a sleek horse that pranced around in the penned in area. "He's your riding partner today."

"Beautiful horse." Kent noticed most of the horses ran free in the field. He stepped to the fence and propped a foot on the rail.

"Hero has a lot of experience with first time riders."

"Good deal."

"An old pro. He was the horse I used when I taught Abby."

"He's a big guy."

Sam nodded. "Hero is a gelding. In layman's terms that means he's a castrated male."

"Ouch." Kent had to laugh.

"Geldings are easier to work with because they have a calm nature. Not flighty like stallions and mares can be."

Sam opened the gate. "First, let's get you acquainted with Hero. He's a real people horse. Once he is familiar with you, he will be putty in your hands."

Kent nodded, then stepped beside Sam and rubbed the gelding's nose. "What kind of horses do you have here?"

"Paso Fino. They are one of the smartest breeds of horses around. Smart, yet docile. Very easy to train."

Hero snuffled toward Kent and he held out his hand. When Hero nudged him with his big brown head, and rubbed a jowl against his shoulder, Kent felt confident he'd be riding with Carrie and her family sooner than later.

After Sam gathered the riding gear, Kent watched him slide the saddle pad into place, then hoist the saddle on the horse's back. Kent noticed that though Hero angled his head toward Sam, the horse did not seem to mind at all.

"Okay, time to get in the saddle." Sam raised a brow. "Ready?"

"Yep. Let's do this."

"Always stand on the horse's left side to mount. Then you'll put your left foot in the stirrup."

Kent stepped to the designated position.

"Now place your weight on your left foot and step up to a standing position. Your right leg will be hanging next to your left."

Kent sucked in a breath and hoisted himself up until he was in the position Sam suggested. It felt odd.

"Good job. Now swing your right leg up and over the horse's rump. But be careful not to accidently kick him. Then sit down in the saddle as gently as possible."

Kent followed Sam's explicit directions and found himself perched in the saddle on top of Hero.

"Now secure your right foot in the stirrup. Center the ball of your foot on the stirrup, not your toe or heel."

Kent wiggled his right foot into the stirrup. "I made it."

"Yep." Sam handed Kent the reins. "Hold the ends of the reins in your left hand just in front of the saddle, but keep them loose. Now sit deep and relaxed in the saddle, and keep the reins slightly loose. You don't want to pull back on Hero's mouth."

"Gotcha."

"Now give him a gentle squeeze with your lower legs and that signals him to walk." Sam chuckled. "And I emphasize gentle. Don't want him to take off running. At least not just yet."

Kent laughed. "That's for sure." Always adept at following directions, he was careful to do just as

Sam instructed. In no time he was bobbing up and down on Hero's back while Sam stayed close beside the horse. "Are you supposed to bounce around so much?"

"I hear that from all beginners." Sam threw his head back and laughed. "Trust me, in time you'll learn to go with the flow and won't bounce so much."

"If you say so."

"Sit up tall, hold your head up straight, and look between your horse's ears, not at the ground."

Kent jerked upright and aimed his eyes between Hero's ears. He hadn't realized he was slumping slightly until Sam commented.

"One more thing to remember." Sam gently touched Kent's leg. "Try not to squeeze repeatedly with your legs once the horse is walking. Keep your legs long, quiet, and with weight firmly down in your heels."

Kent nodded. "Lots to learn."

"For your first lesson, you are doing great. Actually, better than most."

"If you say so."

"I say so. Now it's time to let Hero know you want him to stop walking. So here's what you do; pull back gently on the reins. Ever so gentle. Do not jerk. And don't keep pulling at them like you're pulling a rope. Instead, alternate tightening and releasing the pressure. Remember, the bit is in his mouth, and his mouth is sensitive."

Kent eased back on the reins, then Hero stopped.

"Now release the reins and give his neck a nice pat as a reward."

Then after explicit directives from his mentor, Kent dismounted and landed on the ground beside Hero.

He smiled. "And that wraps up my first lesson."

"It does." Sam gave a thumbs up. "You've learned a lot today, and I'm impressed how well you've done."

Kent was glad he'd decided to take Sam up on the riding lesson. But more than anything else, he enjoyed his time with Sam. He felt they had formed a bond today. Carrie's family was as receptive to him as she was.

"One more thing." Sam glanced at his feet. "If you're going to do a lot of riding, I suggest you splurge on good riding boots. They work much better in the stirrups and will give you a better grip."

Kent nodded. "I'll definitely do that."

He walked beside Sam while he led the gelding toward the stable.

Kent admired Sam. To think a physician would also be a skilled horse trainer boggled his mind. Obviously, Sam proved his efficiency at a variety of things. After all, he'd worked a year as a maintenance man and from what Kent had heard, Sam had done a great job at that too.

Back in the barn, Kent watched Sam pull off the saddle. Hero sauntered to the water trough, dipped his head, and took a long drink.

"It won't be long until you'll be a better rider than me."

"I doubt that." Kent laughed. "But it will be nice to be able to ride along with you guys."

* * *

Saturday afternoon, after his first riding experience, Kent unlocked his apartment door and when he stepped through the doorway, he noticed he whistled a tune. *Don't Worry Be Happy*, a melody he recognized. He never whistled before, but he'd never felt so upbeat. He'd spent most of the day with Carrie's family, really getting to know them. Now he would get to spend the evening with Carrie.

The atmosphere at Sam's had been intoxicating with smiles, bursts of laughter and lots of hugging. Watching the closeness and easy camaraderie between the Dennison family had made his heart melt.

He crossed the living room and padded into the kitchen which was rectangle like a dollar bill, edged with stainless steel appliances, white cabinets, black granite counter top and a double sink. Beyond was a very small cubby-hole for a stacked washer and dryer, and the back door.

He opened the refrigerator to find milk and half-and-half, a six-pack of Diet Dr. Pepper, and apples and oranges in plastic bags. Deli lunch meat and pepper-jack cheese were in the meat drawer. He grabbed a diet soda and stepped outside to the small deck, complete with black canvas director's chairs around a teak table and a Hestan propane grill, which he hadn't used yet. He'd have to invite Carrie to join him for grilled steak and corn-on-the-cob soon. She had invited him for dinner tonight, and he counted down the minutes until he would see her. She hadn't told him what the menu consisted of, but he wouldn't care if she served cheese sticks and apple slices. Just being with her would satisfy him. When he was away from her, he missed her with every cell in his body.

Memories of today's events slipped down, and he grabbed them. He let them play through his mind, like a television re-run, while he sipped from the Dr. Pepper can. He'd not only grown closer to Abby's family, but thanks to Sam he'd done pretty darn good with the horse too.

He went back inside, stepped into the shower, washing away the lingering aroma of horses. Then time to see Carrie. He felt strangely as if he'd lived his entire life for this moment.

CHAPTER SEVENTEEN

The apartment was pin quiet by the time Carrie got home from work. She clicked on the television, turning the volume low. She flipped channels until she found a repeat of Law & Order. Though she wasn't a big fan of TV, she liked the background noise, the familiarity, the flicker of the dim light. When she did take the time to watch a show, she usually opted for one of the older shows on COZI TV. She'd be sure to turn the set off when Kent arrived for dinner. She did not want any distractions.

When she stepped into the kitchen, the aroma from the crockpot wafted over her, making her stomach growl. She lifted the lid and peeked inside. Everything looked good. She opened the utensil drawer, picked up a fork and inserted it into the meat, so tender it tried to fall apart.

After a quick shower, she dried off, blow-dried her hair, then slipped on jeans and a vanilla cream peasant blouse.

After she applied foundation, a touch of blush, and a swipe of lip balm, she slipped her feet into the new beige Hey Dudes she'd purchased last week. Stepping in front of the full-length mirror mounted on the back of the bedroom door, she checked her image. Not bad, she thought.

Walking out of her bedroom, she felt an extra bounce in her step and a smile on her face.

In the kitchen, she gathered the ingredients for the charcuterie board that was on the agenda for tonight. Emmy had taught her how to create a fantastic assortment of goodies that not only looked appetizing, but would also catch the eye. Carrie had witnessed several masterpieces laid out on a board by her sister.

Carrie wanted hers to be on a much smaller scale, ideal for two. Simple, yet functional, she didn't want to overdo since this was just the appetizer. Her entrée was simmering in the crockpot, beef roast, small Yukon gold potatoes, and baby carrots.

She rolled slices of prosciutto and salami into circles, secured them with a toothpick, and laid them of the board. Next, she made several cubes of Colby and Gouda cheese, and laid them in between the meat. One baby food jar placed in the center held Dijon mustard, while another held green olives. Pumpkin seeds and almonds in a two-sided wood nut bowl were placed to the right of the meat and cheese. Last she snaked a stack of crackers like a vein, through the board. Breadsticks stood tall in a mason jar.

Carrie made a mental note to ask Kent tonight how he liked her nick-name Samantha had let out of the bag today. Abby had called and said she'd been horrified when Samantha blurted out, 'he's Boo Boo's hunk'. The hunk didn't bother Carrie. Kent had to know he was good-looking. She was sure he'd been told that more than once.

Her thoughts were interrupted by a tap on her door. She flew to the living room, clicked the TV off, then straightened her blouse and headed to the door.

* * *

Kent paced back and forth, ready to go long before time to head Carrie's way. She'd said to arrive at 6 PM. Getting there at 5 would not be kosher. And just downright rude. To occupy his time, and because he hadn't called in a week, he punched in his mom's memory number. It went to voice mail. Dang.

He sauntered into the living room, plopped down in the recliner, picked up his iPad and checked social media. This held his attention for approximately five minutes. Laying down the tablet, he hauled himself up, grabbed his phone and googled 'nearest flower shop from this address'. When Google replied, he headed out the door, slid behind the wheel of his jeep and headed the five miles to the nearest florist. By the time he'd purchased one lone item and paid the clerk, it was time to navigate to Carrie's. On the drive he justified his purchase, telling himself he wasn't cheap. He hadn't wanted to go overboard and show up with a dozen red roses. That would just be way too obvious.

He looked at his watch when he exited his vehicle and walked along the sidewalk to Carrie's front door. Two minutes till six. He gave himself a pat on the back for such good timing.

"Hello, beautiful." Kent handed Carrie a single red rose when she opened her apartment door.

She smiled, the fullness of her mouth like a magnet to his eyes. Although he did make an effort not to stare, he had to fight a sudden urge to pull her into his arms and lavish her with kisses.

When she reached for the rose and lifted the flower to her face, he heard her inhale deeply. Her button nose crinkled, making her look cute, rather than her usual gorgeous.

"Thank you. It is beautiful." She stepped back and added, "Please come in."

Kent stepped across the room on the heels of Carrie. His heart felt light and hopeful; his belly full of glittering monarchs. Her dark hair bounced and glistened in the weak rays of the late afternoon sun that spilled through the windows.

"Mmm, something smells good," he said.

He watched her pull a vase from a nearby cabinet, filling it with water. She added the rose, then placed it in the middle of the kitchen table. He was impressed she was using the rose as a centerpiece. The lady at the flower shop had told him that giving a single rose symbolized the giving of your heart. Since Carrie's sister owned a flower shop, he hoped his nurse understood the message he was sending her.

"Help yourself while I put the main course on the table." She tossed him her million-dollar smile and motioned him toward a tray situated on the counter.

"This looks delicious." Kent used tongs and placed a variety of appetizers on a small plate. "You're not only beautiful, now I'm discovering the homemaker side of you."

Kent watched, fascinated while two dark patches of pink appeared in the center of Carrie's cheeks. She blushed, he thought, and his heart swelled. He loved that about her. Actually, he loved everything about her.

"What can I do to help?"

He leaned his back against the counter, and his gaze dropped to her mouth again, bringing back memories of the first kiss. When their lips had met, there'd been an explosion of sensation. By the time he'd come up for air, he'd felt drunk on her. Kent pulled his gaze from her lips and reminded himself they were in her apartment. Alone. He did not want to do anything that might compromise their relationship.

"You're the guest." She smiled, then pointed to the kitchen table. "Just have a seat and enjoy your drink and appetizer while I get the rest of the meal in place."

He took a swallow of tea, then scooted out a chair and sat down. He watched her transfer a roast and vegetables to a tray and place it on the table.

She retraced her steps and took hot rolls out of the oven, then delivered the rest of her bounty to the table.

After she joined him at the table she said, "Would you like to ask the blessing?"

He brought prayer hands together, then bowed his head and said a short prayer.

"Now lets dig in," Carrie said.

"We've never talked about it, but I assume you are a Believer."

She nodded. "I was brought up in a Christian home. I accepted the Lord into my heart and was baptized when I was twelve. Though I haven't always been faithful to God, He has never been unfaithful to me."

"I surrendered my life to the Lord when I was in high school. Shortly before Mom got her cancer diagnosis."

"God's timing is always perfect." She passed him the tray of steaming meat.

"Always." He forked roast beef on his plate. It was so tender he couldn't get a true slice. Just the way he liked it. "Looking back, that's all that got me through that period of my life."

The more he learned about this beautiful lady, the more intrigued he became and the more his heart yearned to be with her. He knew she played a major role in his future, and he'd never let her slip away. Not if he had anything to say about it. He smiled when his mind drifted to a black Labrador Retriever leaping through the air, plowing into Carrie. He owed that big dog a huge thank-you.

"I heard you did great with your riding lesson."

"I took to it like a pro." He laughed. "Seriously, it went well. Sam is a great instructor."

"And, I found out that a little birdie told you I have a nickname."

"Oh yeah, Boo Boo. That's cute. What's the story behind it?"

She explained the meaning of her nickname. "And my sisters won't let me live it down."

"They love you."

"Yes, I'm definitely blessed."

They lingered over the meal and Kent enjoyed the light banter they shared through the evening.

Carrie held up the basket of hot rolls and extended it toward him. "Care for another?"

"No, I couldn't hold another bite. I'm so full I could burst." Kent laughed.

"No room for dessert?"

Kent paused. He placed a hand on his abdomen. "Depends. What is it?"

"Something light. Homemade custard."

"You have got to be kidding me."

She shook her head. "No. Why?"

"Custard is my all-time favorite. Mom used to make it especially for me because no one else in the family cared for it that much."

"So, surely you can at least taste it. See how it compares to your mother's."

He smiled. "I'm sure I'll do a lot more than taste it once you sit it before me."

Carrie stood and walked to the refrigerator. She returned to the table and set two ramekins down. "It's my favorite too."

Kent spooned a bite of custard past his lips.

Flavors exploded in his mouth, and his taste buds sent positive signals to his brain. He quickly compared it to his mother's custard. "This is every bit as good as Mom's. You have outdone yourself."

Her eyes lit up at his compliment and he could see how pleased she was.

After he'd gobbled down every last bite, he said, "Now I'm beyond stuffed. But it was worth it. Everything was delicious. You could be a chef."

"Thank you. I learned from the best. Mom is a great cook."

"She trained you well."

"I like to cook. Don't really do much now. But when I lived at home, I did a lot of meal preparation for my family."

Kent stood. "Let me help you with the dishes." He gathered his plate and utensils and took them to the sink.

"Okay, if you insist." Carrie joined him at the sink,

"Would you like to come to my apartment for dinner. Say Sunday?"

"I'd love to."

"I'm pretty good on the grill. How does steak and roasting ears sound?"

Carrie opened the dishwasher then looked into his eyes. "Sounds perfect." He noticed she kept her gaze on him for several beats before she looked away.

Kent watched her place the dishes on the rack. He wondered if she had any idea how appealing she looked? He stared long enough it caught her attention.

"What? she asked.

He shook his head. "Like I told you before, I just like looking at you."

"You're not too hard to take yourself." She ran the tip of her tongue over her lower lip.

He wanted to kiss her. Really wanted to. Like at the stable. But since they were alone in her apartment he held back. He placed both hands on her shoulders. Leaned in and kissed her on the cheek. "I had a wonderful time tonight. I hope we can have many more good times together."

She nodded. "You must have read my mind."

* * *

Sunday evening Carrie rang Kent's doorbell.

When he opened the door he shot her the grin that always melted her heart.

"Come in, beautiful," he said. "Dinner will be ready in about an hour. Let me pull a couple steaks from the fridge, make us a cup of hot chocolate, then we can sit in the living room and visit."

Fifteen minutes later, Carrie was where she'd wanted to be all day. With her legs curled under her, she wrapped her fingers around a cup of steaming cocoa and nestled against Kent's side. The sound of wind pummeling the house was a central Florida serenade and enhanced her contentment.

"Cocoa's delicious." Carrie set the cup on the coffee table. "It's homemade, I can tell."

He grinned as if she'd gifted him with an early birthday present. "Half milk, half cream. That's my secret."

She mentally added the calories in her head and the number shocked her. But she didn't care. Tonight she was determined to eat and drink whatever she felt like. No holding back.

"Forecasters say we're going to get dumped on tonight," he said.

A ripple of excitement ran up her spine when he linked her fingers with his and brought their joined hands to his lips. The soft kiss made her hand tingle.

"It'll be a good night for sleeping."

"With the windows open." Kent's blue eyes sparkled. "Not only can you hear the wind and rain, if it's coming from the south, you'll get a mist on your face from time to time."

Carrie laughed at the memories of a fine mist spraying gently over her face. "Oh, yes, I love that." Each time she was with Kent, she discovered more and more commonalities they shared. "When I lived at home, Mom always scolded me for the damp sheets she'd discover the morning after a good rain."

"I remember more than one chewing out my brother and I got from Mom."

Kent leaned forward, resting his muscular forearms on his thighs as he studied her. "I hate to end this conversation, but if I don't get the steaks on the grill, we'll be eating peanut butter sandwiches."

"Well then, let's tackle the steaks." She wouldn't care if all they had were sandwiches as long as she could have them with Kent.

Later, after the meal was over and the dishes done, Carrie motioned toward the living room. "I see you like jigsaw puzzles."

"Yeah." He took her arm and navigated her to the table in the corner of the room which donned a partially put together puzzle.

Carrie picked up the box and perused the directions. "This is a 1000-piece puzzle, which means its four times as difficult as one that has 500 pieces."

"That's right."

"And look at the color gradations. This is one challenging puzzle."

"Are you into jigsaws too?"

"Am I ever." Carrie laughed and picked up a knob. "My sisters always had a puzzle up and going when they were home. At first when I tried to help, I was too little to really understand. But they were patient. Finally, when I grew older, and knew what I was doing, I tried so hard to be as proficient as they were. The Dennison siblings are very competitive. Detail-oriented and problem solvers."

"It's relaxing. Fitting the knobs into the holes improves visual-spatial reasoning."

Carrie nodded and placed the knob into a hole.

"Way to go." Kent's mouth turned up into a smile. "I've been looking for that piece for two days." He stepped into the kitchen, brought another chair to the small puzzle table and motioned for her to sit.

Carrie plopped down in the seat.

She watched Kent rub his hands together while he slid into the seat across from her. "Are you ready for this?"

"Bring it on." Carrie laughed. And for the next hour they worked diligently side-by-side.

CHAPTER EIGHTEEN

Carrie hopped out of the shower and blow-dried her hair, made a fishtail braid, then coiled the braid into a bun before pinning it securely in place with lots of bobby pins.

She painstakingly applied make up, then eyed the outfit she'd laid on the bed. She wanted to look just right tonight. Sara's graduation party was incentive enough, but she knew in her heart the main reason she'd fussed with her attire was Kent. She wanted to look especially nice for him.

The new strapless, wide leg jumpsuit, nude in color with a tie at the waist, lay on the bed next to the matching cropped blazer. She slipped on the outfit, then looked in the mirror, pulling her shoulders back and straightening the tie.

Then she retrieved the yellow gold layered

necklace, featuring a small round diamond on the upper chain and a delicate oval pearl on the lower chain, and fastened the clasp behind her neck. She massaged her earlobe with forefinger and thumb, while she peered into her jewelry box. Finally, she opted for the simple but classic gold hoop earrings.

She sat on the edge of the bed, slipped on her three-inch nude open toed heels, revealing her freshly manicured nails. For her left wrist she put on a gold toned watch with a large rectangular mother of pearl dial. She looked in the mirror again. Satisfied she looked well put together, she picked up her simple cream-colored clutch so she could carry the subtle pink lipstick that complimented the natural look of her carefully applied make-up. Then she headed to the living room to wait for her date.

Fifteen minutes later, when Carrie opened her front door and saw Kent standing there, she took a startled step back. As handsome as he'd looked in the past, dressed in his suit at work, tonight he stole her breath. The man that stood before her tonight looked beyond dapper.

He wore a crisp white long sleeve button-up dress shirt, with the two top buttons undone. The navy blue fitted suit, tailored slim from the shoulders down to his ankles, wrapped around him like a glove. The cognac brown belt with a gold buckle matched the Italian leather slip on shoes, with no socks, perfectly. On his wrist he sported a sleek stainless steel and yellow gold two-toned watch.

"Good evening, beautiful." Kent's white even teeth flashed in an approving smile. "You look terrific."

"You as well."

Kent offered his arm and Carrie linked hers through it. She felt like Cinderella being led to the carriage by Prince Charming.

Carrie carefully settled into Kent's jeep. Not only did he look good, he smelled even better. His aftershave was subtle, but hints of woodsy lime wafted over her, eddied in her brain, half dizzying her. She didn't know if she'd remain conscious sitting so close to this unbelievably perfect man.

"I'm looking forward to this evening," Kent said.

Kent's husky voice warmed her heart. She could tell he was smiling, just like he always did, before she took in his face. When he turned the key in the ignition the engine sprang to life.

"Oh, me too." Carrie was excited that Kent was accompanying her to Sara's big blow-out graduation celebration. Sam and Abby had gone all out to make this a special night for Sam's oldest daughter.

"Where's the big bang going to be?"

"Wellswood Civic Center." Carrie called out the address.

She watched him GPS it into his phone.

"They've gone all out, huh? Hired a band. Catered dinner."

"Sam wants to do something special for Sara." Carrie tucked a strand of hair behind her ear. "Her mother won't be there and that breaks Sam's heart for his daughter."

"Hard to believe a parent could be so uncaring."

"Sad, but true. She hasn't seen Sara in four

years."

"Bummer." Kent shook his head, then took Carrie's hand. "It's a blessing she has Sam and Abby to dote on her."

A few minutes later, Carrie let Kent take her arm and escort her through the doorway of the Civic Center. Peeking at the group of people who had gathered to celebrate with Sara, she felt Kent's eyes on her, and she wondered what was going on inside his head. She'd caught him gazing at her a little too long more than once tonight.

"Thanks for coming." Sara's long, slender fingers wrapped around Carrie's arm. "You look gorgeous. I love, love, love your outfit." Sara's attention turned to Kent then she whistled softly. "And you. You look beyond gorgeous."

"Talk about gorgeous, you're the one catching everyone's eye tonight, right Kent?"

"Absolutely," Kent agreed.

"You guys are just too cool." The corners of Sara's mouth turned upward, then she raced away to join her friends by the buffet.

"She's having a good time." Kent smiled.

He laid a hand on Carrie's shoulder, causing warmth to shower over her.

Carrie's eyes scanned the room, admiring the decorations. Mom and Abby had done a great job as usual. She turned and found Kent's gaze aimed at her again, a strange emotion lingering behind his blue eyes. Being caught off guard by his penetrating look, she felt heat rush to her cheeks.

"Hello? Earth calling Carrie." Abby's voice brought Carrie back to the present. "Come on, you guys, grab some appetizers and punch."

"Shall we?" Kent asked.

"Yeah." The word left her lips weakly. What was it about this man that made her go shaky? Fighting to keep her body under control, she inhaled a long deep breath.

After they finished a small plate of appetizers and a cup of orange sherbet punch, Carrie let Kent take her arm and guide her across the room.

Kent towered over her short height, unusually quiet and peering at her in a way that made her shift on her feet. Why did he keep looking at her like that? she wondered.

Silence settled between them, bringing to Carrie's attention they were no longer surrounded by the crowd that had gathered in front of the buffet. Instead, the murmur of voices accompanied with a mellow tune came all the way from the other side of the room.

"Dance with me." Kent's voice sounded husky.

She noticed it wasn't a question. He offered his hand, letting it hang close to hers.

Carrie accepted his offer, letting his large palm wrap around hers.

Kent pulled her gently behind him, and her legs shook with a weird mixture of anticipation and nervousness. His hand was warm and firm against hers, and it made her feel tingly deep in her stomach.

When they reached the designated dancing area, he stopped walking, then turned and stepped close – so very close – to her. He draped his arms around her waist, and she felt a shock of electricity shoot across her body originating from the points where his hands rested on her back. Her breath caught, and something heavy and solid dropped to the bottom of her stomach.

Carrie swallowed hard, tilted her head back so she could see Kent's face. She placed both hands on his chest and couldn't help but notice how firm and toned it felt under her fingers. Only then did she let him pull her close. Her petite frame immediately cradled in his much larger one.

A heartbeat later, they were moving to the music, bodies pressed close. Kent's motions were sure, directing, while hers felt stiff and incompliant. She released a breath and tried to relax her limbs. She tried to focus on the mechanics of dancing and calm the heat that raged inside her.

Kent spun her in a circle with a swift motion and pressed her against him one more time, making her pulse pummel. She was certain he could feel her heart pounding against his chest.

The music played on. Slow, perfect for swaying and forgetting about everything other than the smooth rhythm. Ideal for getting lost in the total peace that being safe in someone's arms could bring. But the more they swayed, the further she was from feeling anything that resembled peace. Not when Kent felt so warm next to her.

She chided herself for acting like a high-school girl at the prom. She needed to calm down, enjoy the moment with this man that was so handsome it hurt to look at him.

Kent's diligent and smooth motions spun her one more time to the soft tune. Then the song ended.

They stepped apart. She looked up into his ocean-blue eyes and he tossed her a wink.

"I like dancing with you," he said.

His voice low and gravelly, said more than his words intimated, and Carrie felt heat rush to her cheeks yet again.

"Can I get you some punch?" Kent asked.

"I'd love some."

While she watched him walk away, she saw Abby heading her way.

"Oh my gosh." Abby fanned herself with an open hand. "If only you could have seen the look on Kent's face when you guys were dancing, you would have fallen over."

"Almost fell over anyway." Carrie squeezed her sister's arm. "It was so intense I couldn't breathe."

"You both have it bad for each other."

"I sure felt sparks between us."

"I thought I was going to have to call the Fire Department."

Carrie laughed. "He is so darn handsome. I can hardly look at him without drooling."

"Here he comes. I'm gonna give you two some privacy."

"Hey, Abby." Kent handed Carrie a cup of punch. "Don't rush off on my account."

"I've got to mingle, you know."

"This is a great party." Kent's smile spread across his face. "One Sara will never forget. She's so blessed to have you and Sam."

Abby's face seemed to glow. "We were happy to do it for her. She's come a long way since I first met her. I love her like my own now."

Carrie watched Sam amble over with a crooked smile creasing his face. He greeted her and Kent, then he took Abby's hand and said, "How about a dance?"

"Mingle will have to wait." Abby laughed and walked hand in hand to the dance floor with her husband.

The next song was a fast tune. Carrie looked at Kent. "Can you twist?"

"Is the Pope Catholic?"

He nodded toward the dance floor and off they went.

The night ended sooner than Carrie wanted. If she'd had her way, she would have spent several more hours with Kent. But since it was one o'clock Sunday morning, she admitted it was time to graciously let things come to an end.

There's always tomorrow, she thought. And she hoped for many tomorrows with Kent.

CHAPTER NINETEEN

Monday morning Carrie caught a glimpse of herself in the mirror. She stopped in her tracks and took a long look. It wasn't just her imagination, a glow lit up her image and she knew why. She smiled at her reflection and said a silent thank you for the day Kent entered her life, teaching her to trust in love again.

She showered, dressed for work, and thirty minutes later found herself at Tampa General, early as usual. She resisted the urge to head to Kent's office. They had talked about keeping work and personal separate. He didn't want a conflict-of-interest complaint ruining their relationship.

Relationship. He'd actually referred to what they had as a relationship.

"You look cheerful this morning." Brenda

walked behind the nurse's counter and picked up an iPad.

"Aren't I always?"

Carrie saw questions in her friend's eyes.

"Not this cheerful."

"Ah, you're hurting my feelings."

"Could this have anything to do with your date with Kent Saturday?"

Carrie shrugged.

"I see you're going to make me beg you for information."

"You mean the graduation bash?" Carrie smiled and feigned innocence.

Brenda swatted her on the arm. "Out with it. I want details."

"We danced."

"And?"

"And what can I say?" Carrie placed her hands on each side of her very warm face. "It felt so good to be held in his arms."

"You're blushing." Brenda laughed. "You really are blushing. This sounds like things are getting serious between the two of you."

"Well, it sure felt that way Saturday night. He's such a good dancer. I thought I was an okay dancer, but compared to him, I'm a klutz."

"You've got it bad, my friend." Brenda fanned her face with an open hand. "Will I be hearing wedding bells in the future."

"Things haven't progressed that far." Carrie brought her hands to her chest, shaped them into a heart. "I think I'm falling in love with him."

"You think?" Brenda's eyes grew wide. "Yeah,

right."

Carrie chuckled. "I have to admit I do love him."

"I knew that from day one. I think you did too."

"That man blew into my life like a hurricane, and I haven't been the same since."

"I am so happy for you."

Carrie took her spot behind the nurse's station, ready for report. She saw Linda and Gwen round the corner and head toward the counter.

"Well, how'd it go Saturday night with Mr. hunk-of-all-time?" Gwen and Linda asked simultaneously.

"Shhhh." Carrie brought her finger to her lips, and nodded toward the night nurse approaching them. "I'll tell you later."

After report, Carrie glanced to the right and saw Kent headed toward them. He had the profile of Adonis. She wondered if she'd ever get used to his good looks.

"Good morning, ladies." Kent gave his million-dollar smile to the group. Then he leaned close and said words meant only for her ears. "Shoot me a text when you clock out for lunch and if my board meeting is over, I'll meet you in the cafeteria. If you want."

Carrie nodded. "I want."

He threw her a wink before heading toward the elevator.

"He is so into you, Carrie." Linda shook her head. "I thought he was gonna kiss you right in front of us."

Carrie shrugged. "Wouldn't have hurt my feelings."

"No kidding," Gwen said. "I'd let that hunk kiss me anywhere, anytime."

"Should I be jealous?" Carrie laughed. She knew Gwen was all talk. She wouldn't cheat on her guy, but that never stopped her from looking.

"Are you kidding?" Gwen's eyebrows danced up and down. "If I had half a chance, I'd let him whisk me away in a heartbeat. Just saying."

"I hate to break this man fest up, but there's work to do." Brenda's voice turned gruff, but her smile told Carrie she wasn't upset with her nurses.

After two admissions, Carrie had her patients settled in and comfortable. Looking at the oversized clock in the hallway, she noticed it was time for lunch.

She pulled her phone from her scrubs pocket and sent Kent a text, *I'm on my way to the cafeteria.*

The lunchroom was busy as usual when she walked along the food bar, choosing a combo sandwich and baked chips today. Filled tray in hand, she scanned the area, hoping she'd get a glimpse of her handsome CEO. But to her dismay she never spotted Kent. He'd mentioned he had a Board of Directors meeting, and she assumed the meeting ran long. She hauled her food to the outside seating area and found an empty two-seat table near the windows. That way she could keep an eye out for Kent.

She slid into the seat, unwrapped her sandwich and took a bite. Still reeling from time spent dancing with Kent Saturday night at Sara's party, she had to pinch herself to make sure it had actually happened. The way he'd looked at her and held her while he guided her across the room lingered in her mind. She couldn't shake the notion that he might actually feel about her the same way she felt about him.

She took another bite of the sandwich, enjoying the tasty combo of meat, cheese, pickles and mustard. After she chewed and swallowed, she chased down the bite with a sip of sweet tea. When she turned and glanced toward the window, she spotted Kent with three other men dressed in suits. She pulled in a breath. Board meeting must be over.

Just then he glanced toward the window, threw up a hand, waved.

Carrie waved back and smiled.

She saw Kent lean forward, spoke to the men, then he turned and headed her way.

"Hey, Kent."

"Hey, beautiful."

"Long meeting?"

Kent nodded. "Three of the Board Members asked me to join them for lunch."

"Go ahead. I'm about to finish up here."

"Carrie, you know if I had my choice…" He tapped his chest on a spot over his heart. "I'd rather spend the time with you."

She met his gaze. "I know."

"Well, I gotta go and join the others. But I will be talking to you soon."

Carrie finished her sandwich, drank the last of her tea and, after she'd disposed of her tray and trash, she headed back to her unit. But not before she took one last glance at Kent seated with the other men. The four of them looked so dignified.

However, none of them could begin to measure up to her handsome executive.

She spent the afternoon checking on the new admissions and administering pain meds as needed. One patient's IV line infiltrated, and Carrie gathered a new set-up and had the line going in record time, even for her.

Before Carrie had a chance to check her missed calls, it was time to leave for the day.

She stepped into the elevator and punched first floor. She pulled her phone from her purse, then swiped the screen. There were three calls from unknown numbers which she immediately deleted. When she noticed the missed call from Mom, the elevator doors opened. She fell into a seat in the lobby and checked voicemail.

Mom's tearful message was hard to understand the first time so she replayed it. This time the news hit her like a slap to the face.

Carrie hit the memory number for Mom. When her mother answered, Carrie said, "Why in the world didn't you let me know sooner?"

Mom's voice sounded soft and muted. "Dad didn't want to worry you."

"Well, that didn't work out so well, did it?"

She heard her mom breathing into the phone, but she remained quiet.

"I just got off work. I'll be at your house in an hour."

"No. Please wait until tomorrow. Your father has had a rough day. He went to bed and is sound asleep."

Carrie huffed out a breath. "Okay, but I will be

there first thing in the morning." Carrie was beyond upset with her parents. Why hadn't they let her know sooner?

She rushed through the hospital doors and quick stepped to her car.

She had to see Kent.

A few minutes later Carrie parked her car in Kent's parking garage. When she pressed his doorbell, she continued to process the disturbing voicemail she'd received from her mother.

He opened the door and she could see the questions that flew across his eyes.

"Sorry to just pop in. I didn't want to be alone tonight."

"Not a problem."

She was deep in thought as he led her into the kitchen and motioned to a chair.

"Everything okay?" Kent asked.

"Oh, yeah. Sure."

"Carrie, I. . ." He paused.

Carrie saw understanding lining his face when he went quiet. She couldn't fool him.

"Actually, things really aren't okay."

"You want to talk about it?"

"No. Yes." She shook her head. "I just got a tearful voice mail from my mother. She said Dad's doctor called last week and told him he has melanoma. Last week, mind you. And she's just now letting me know. He already has an appointment set up to have the melanoma surgically removed."

"You never knew?" Kent's eyebrows lifted.

"I knew he'd had an excisional biopsy done on

his forehead. I went with them for that appointment."

Kent remained silent. She realized he was giving her time to process her thoughts.

"Apparently he was referred to a dermatologist who ordered a lymph node biopsy." Suddenly a ball of fear gripped her rib cage with cold fingers. She knew all too well that melanoma was notorious for spreading to lymph nodes. If that happened it could be really bad news.

Kent waved a hand toward her phone. "Call her if you want."

"I did, as soon as I got the voice mail. I told her I was on my way to Orlando. She said not to come, it's too late and Dad had already gone to bed. It isn't even seven o'clock and he's already down for the night."

Kent shook his head, resting a hand on her arm. "She's right. Tomorrow's another day."

"And I don't care what she says." Carrie glanced at Kent's hand, then laid her hand on top of his and gave it a squeeze. "I'm heading to Orlando tomorrow."

"I'm sure they will be glad to have you there for support."

"Well, I wish they'd let me be a support when they first learned about the melanoma."

"Ah, don't be upset with them. Parents don't want to worry their children."

Carrie blew out an audible sigh. "That's what Mom said."

"Your mom and dad would never shut you out, you know that."

Carrie nodded. "I can't lose my dad. He's always been the rock in our family."

"I understand."

Of course he understood Carrie thought. She flashed on Kent's description of how devastated he'd been when he thought he would lose his mother.

"I hate cancer."

"Ditto," Kent agreed.

She watched Kent reach across the table and give her arm a tender pat.

Her eyes met his and she let her gaze linger on his mouth and tried to will him to kiss her.

She sensed he felt the crackle of energy because when he turned slightly in his seat his eyes grew round. He tilted his head and seemed to study her.

"I'm usually not impulsive." Carrie stood and moved around the table so she stood beside Kent. "But I need your strength tonight." She placed her hand on one of his broad shoulders. "I know we've talked about taking things slow. About not blurring the lines between work and personal. But I need your arms around me. I need to be close to you."

"Carrie. . ." He stood and lifted one of those capable hands and laid it on top of hers. "You had something difficult happen tonight, and I want to be here for you. And while I don't want to walk away, I want this to be for the right reasons."

She stared into those electric blue eyes then knew, as cliché as it sounded, she could get lost there. She wanted to get lost there.

"I'm making the decision because I want to. Because I need your strength. Not just because of the disturbing news. But because I.. ."

Carrie paused when Kent held up a finger to silence her. The hand that lay over the top of hers shifted, lifting to cup the tender skin at the back of her neck. He exerted very gentle pressure, pulling her closer to him as he stood.

"It's not because of Dad." The words had barely left her lips before his arm went around her, and his mouth closed over hers. Her heart, heavy a second earlier, gave a leap when their lips met. The floor beneath her gave away.

She couldn't recall ever being kissed like that. Sweet, gentle kisses that teased and tantalized. Steamy kisses that had her heart rate skyrocketing and her blood flowing hot in her veins.

The shock – and the very real fear – that she had felt at her mother's voicemail faded away.

And as she sunk into the kiss, planting her free hand on top of Kent's other shoulder, Carrie knew she loved this man with her whole heart.

CHAPTER TWENTY

Carrie woke up the next morning after a restless night. Her first thought was Dad's diagnosis. She closed her eyes, hoping it wasn't true. She made herself open her eyes, then looked around the bedroom for a minute, orienting herself. She loved this room with walls painted a light gray and the room sunny, with a panel of windows on each side. The cool briny breeze and the call of seagulls wafting through the screens usually calmed her nerves. But not this morning.

She pulled in a calming breath, then looked at the time on her phone. She got out of bed and slipped into a red and white T-shirt and jeans, remembering to disable the alarm. She closed the bedroom door and padded to the living room which was furnished with a beige couch, chocolate brown recliner and a gray coffee table. Mounted on the wall above the gas fireplace, was a 50-inch flat TV. An apartment she was proud of, one she loved. Why was she so nostalgic this morning?

Skipping breakfast, she made a beeline for her parent's house. Her thoughts swirled so wildly she had trouble pinning them down. Concern for her father's condition took precedence in her mind. However, she couldn't push thoughts of Kent aside. The tenderness they'd shared. His kisses had left her breathless, caused her knees to tremble. But the closeness they'd shared when the kisses ended, strengthened her resolve to put all her fears aside and let herself trust him enough to give him her heart. He had held her in his gentle arms long after the excitement of the kisses, and she had felt his strength seep throughout her body.

The sight of the familiar driveway pulled her back to the present. She parked her car, sprinted up the sidewalk, unlocked the front door, then flew into the kitchen where Mom and Dad sat, coffee cups in front of them.

"Why in the world didn't you let me go with you to the dermatologist?" Carrie tried to keep criticism at a minimum. However, she heard it oozing from her voice. "You told me you'd call me as soon as you heard from the biopsy. Now I find out the surgery has been scheduled."

Dad's eyes grew wide. "I didn't want to worry my girls. You all have enough going on in your lives as it is. You don't need to worry about an old man."

"You aren't old. Besides, when you reach the

ripe age of ninety, we are still going to worry about you. We love you."

"Aww, baby girl, I love you too. So much it hurts to see you concerned about me."

"Dad. I want to be there when they do the surgery."

"It is scheduled at ten in the morning at Moffitt."

Carrie had heard good reports about Moffitt Cancer Center. Located on the campus of University of South Florida, it was only about fourteen miles from where she lived.

Mom shrugged. "I'm glad someone is going to be in the waiting room with me."

"Of course, I will. Abby and Emmy are going to want to be there, too. Has anybody bothered to let them know what's going on?

"I'll be sure and call them today." Mom wrung her hands.

Carrie shook a forefinger at Dad. "If you do not keep me in the loop, step by step, from now on, I am personally going to throttle you."

Her father laughed.

"I'm serious. Please, Daddy, don't shut me out. Let me be part of this process."

"I told you you'd be in trouble." Mom shot Dad a sharp look. "The girls have a right to know what's going on. Especially with something as serious as cancer."

"It's going to be okay." Dad shrugged. "That dermatologist said my lymph nodes felt normal."

Carrie, determined to get the last word in with her father, said, "Yes, that's what Mom said. And that was very good news. But he also took a biopsy to back up his diagnosis."

When her dad fell silent, Carrie looked down at his wrinkled hands, and her heart filled with an ache she couldn't deny. As bad as she wanted, she couldn't keep her father from aging.

"I understand you want to protect us and keep all the ugly things in life far from us. But I need to ask you a favor."

"What's that?"

"Don't hide things from me. I want to know what's going on. I need to know."

"From now on, I'll keep you updated."

"Don't shut me out again. If you can't tell me something, say so. But don't ignore me."

"I promise."

Dad's focus on her stayed steady and direct, and she could feel the fear he'd had when he received the diagnosis.

The pieces came together on a hard shot of awareness. Her father had kept his daughters in the dark because he was afraid he was going to die.

Tenderness filled her dad's eyes. He held open arms toward Carrie and she stepped into his embrace. He gave her a fierce hug that lasted longer than usual before he released her. She saw moistness in his eyes.

* * *

The waiting room of the surgical outpatient clinic was harshly bright, and the mint green walls were lined with idealized landscapes of foxhunts. Green padded chairs had been arranged in two rectangles, forming rooms without walls. The front section held a handful of people, but the Dennison family had the back to themselves. Wrinkled magazines lay on end tables, ignored in favor of phones. She heard chatter spilling out of a play room situated behind a plexiglass wall.

Carrie sat with her mother and two siblings, praying all would go well with Dad.

"He'll be just fine, right?" Abby asked.

"Yes." Mom's voice barely above a whisper, sounded determined.

Carrie patted her mother's arm.

An older couple shuffled in together, then glanced around as if not sure where to go. The man had a walker with new tennis balls on the bottom, and he walked ahead with concentration. When they took a seat, the woman plastered her gaze on the TV that broadcast closed-captioning news. Would that be Dad and Mom in a few years? She tucked the thought away because she was nowhere near ready to accept such a fate.

Emmy blew her red, swollen nose with a balled-up Kleenex. "If anything were to happen to Dad. . ."

"Don't you dare go there." Tears stung Carrie's eyes. She blinked them back. "Dad is going to be just fine. He's caught it early."

Abby nodded. "And his prognosis is good."

Carrie shifted in the chair. Her mouth had gone dry. It was impossible to wrap her mind around the fact that Dad was lying on an operating table down the hall, behind double doors. Every instinct told her she needed to be in there with him, be at his side. Daddy, please be okay she pleaded silently.

The next couple hours were a blur, and she traveled through them numbly. As a nurse, Carrie was very much aware her father was not in immediate danger. He would not die on the operating table. She knew he would exit the surgical room, a little dazed from the anesthesia, but otherwise unscathed. It was what the doctor would tell them after the procedure that concerned her. Melanoma was the most serious type of skin cancer, could metastasize quickly, even cause death. The exact cause unclear, but exposure to UV radiation from sunlight or tanning lamps increases the risk. Dad had always been an outdoor man. He fished, hunted, and canoed. He loved working in his small garden. Had she harped at him enough about using sun block?

When the pager in Mom's lap beeped, Carrie jumped up.

"He's in recovery and the doctor will meet with us in room A." Mom gathered her purse and stood.

Carrie and her siblings followed Mom through the doorway of room A. The doctor sat at a circular table, a surgical cap hanging loosely around his neck. The smile on his face shot a ping of hopefulness through Carrie's soul.

"The procedure went very well." The surgeon stood, motioned for the family to sit. "I excised the tumor along with a small amount of normal skin around the edges."

"Did you get a clean margin?" Carrie knew the margins would be wider because the diagnosis was already known. The recommended margins vary depending on the thickness of the tumor. Thicker tumors need larger margins, both at the edges and in the depth of the excision.

"Yes. The lab viewed the removed tissue to make sure no cancer cells were left behind at the edges of the skin that I removed." He smiled. "I am very pleased to say the margins are clear."

Mom blew out a breath. "Thank you, Jesus."

"Unlike nonmelanoma skin cancers, which typically do not spread beyond the original tumor site, melanoma can metastasize and affect other parts of the body. So far there are no signs that the cancer has spread. However, I am going to refer Mr. Dennison to an oncologist who will decide if any further steps of treatment are indicated."

Mom spoke up. "Chemotherapy?"

"That is an option. But another option would be do nothing more at this time. The oncologist will be the one to determine the next steps."

Carrie pulled in a breath, blew it out. She prayed her father would not need chemo.

CHAPTER TWENTY-ONE

Kent walked down the long hall at Tampa General, thoughts of Carrie clouding his mind. He turned left and opened his office door. When he slid into his swivel chair, he still savored how good she'd felt in his arms. He'd been overwhelmed with delight when she'd made her aggressive move. How he loved her freedom to let him know she needed him. Even if it only was for that moment.

Since being with Carrie last night, it was impossible for him to forget how her lips had felt on his, how she had worked magic on his heart. And not just his heart, she'd reached deep down into his soul. But today Kent had been plagued by more doubts than he cared to admit. He had never experienced such a strong connection to any woman, never had the unexplainable urge to call a clergy and marry her on the spot.

Of course, his feelings didn't matter. What mattered was that Carrie had needed him. But he couldn't help but wonder, had it happened because she was in pain? She had been worried sick about her father and needed someone to lean on. Someone to hold her and make the scary feelings go away, if only for a moment. He could imagine what sort of emotional turmoil had been going on just beneath her polished veneer.

He remembered the mood swings he had endured during his mother's ordeal with cancer. He had been 17 and just started his senior year in high school when the drama started. And it lasted over a year before the Acuff household regained a normality again. When it seemed like Mom would not make it to her next birthday, he'd felt the ground beneath him give way. He couldn't concentrate. Totally lost his focus. It had been hard to hold on to reality, and Kent had relied on his father and brother for hope and comfort.

Kent sighed. During that difficult time, it seemed the three of them took turns holding each other up. Thank goodness all of them hadn't fallen apart at the same time. When Dad confided to his sons that he felt helpless in his ability to think calmly or to deal with the devastating situation his wife faced, Kent knew he had no choice but to pull himself together. He had to shove his feelings aside and support and encourage, not only his sweet mother, but also his shattered father. He had to be there, not only for Mom, but also Dad. Many a night Kent feared his mother would not wake up the next morning. He'd never let on to his parents how lost he'd been, how sick at heart he'd felt when he had heard Mom heaving and vomiting throughout the night after a treatment. Chemo was a killer.

He thanked God his mother was out of danger now. Active and healthy, strangers would never guess how close to death she came.

A flutter of noise caught Kent's attention. He looked toward his office door just in time to see Ellen peek her head around the corner.

"Hey, lover."

Ellen's voice was barely above a whisper and grated on his last nerve.

"I'm busy, Ellen. I don't have time for an impromptu visit."

"Not even a minute for an old flame?" She shook her head and tsked.

He stood, motioned a dismissive hand toward the door. "Not for anyone."

Ellen bounced toward him and flung both arms tight around his neck. "I bet you could take some time for this."

Kent sucked in a breath and chastised himself for noticing how soft she felt. After all, he hadn't noticed in the past. But in the past, they had never been this close. He wiggled free from her vice-like grip.

She took a half-step back and flicked a piece of lint from the front of his shirt.

"Wow." She slid her palm slowly over his chest. "Nice pecks. It's a shame I never discovered this before."

"Ellen, stop it." With deliberate effort he

clutched her hand, removing it from his body.

She laughed and gave his chest a final pat. Her slender finger moved to his mouth and she traced the outline of his lips. "So soft."

Before he had a chance to move her finger, she leaned in, and he felt her lips graze his. Then in a flash her lips roamed over his and she pressed in, kissing him long and hard.

Pulling free from her clutches, he wiped the back of his hand across his mouth. "I want you to leave."

Ellen crossed her arms over her chest, and he noticed the smug look that outlined her face.

"I am not interested in you. Get that through your head once and for all. We never had make-out sessions like this when we had our few dates and…."

She interrupted him. "Not my fault."

"I refuse to start it now."

She reached for him.

He threw up a hand. "Stop, Ellen. I'm really maxed out."

"Ah, poor baby. It'll be okay."

"I am asking you nicely to leave." He nodded toward the door. "The next time I won't be so nice. If you come back, I hate to do it, but I will call Security. I am not going to deal with you anymore."

Ellen lifted her chin and stomped out in a huff. Before she pushed through the doorway, she turned, eyes blazing and her voice spiteful. "You can't just toss me out. You'll regret this. I promise you it's not over. Not by a long shot."

CHAPTER TWENTY-TWO

Carrie's morning flew by in a flurry of new admissions. She entered her updated notes into the iPad then slipped it into the designated slot at the nurse's station.

"Are you ready to take your lunch break?" Brenda asked.

Carrie nodded. "Yes, if I'm covered. I'm starved."

"You're good to go." Brenda smiled. "I just got back, so take your time. Maybe you'll even run into your hunk in the cafeteria."

"I wish." Carrie laughed, then headed toward the elevator. Just the thought of a possible encounter with her handsome CEO put a zip in her step.

The cafeteria buzzed with chatter. She walked to the unexpected short line at the food counter and picked up a tray, sliding it along the countertop while she considered her options. She scanned the area, but no sign of Kent. She sighed, and proceeded to checkout.

She took her bounty and found a small table in the back. Her choice was a burger and fries because she wasn't in the mood for a healthy salad today. Just as she took her first bite, she noticed someone who looked a lot like her ex heading toward her table. The closer he got, the more her heart pounded. It was Jeff. She felt the blood drain out of her head as she watched him draw closer.

"Hello, Carrie."

It had been ages since she'd heard her name slip from Jeff's mouth. It brought everything flooding back, all the good moments they'd shared, and there had been amazing moments. She'd never forget the naïve joy that came hand in hand with a first love she foolishly thought was going to last forever. But there was a flipside, and a flashbulb memory reminded her of the pain she'd felt when her expectations turned into an ocean of hurt.

"You are sure hard to track down." Jeff slid into the chair opposite her.

"Why are you trying to track me down?" She made air quotes.

"I've got to talk to you."

Carrie pulled in a breath and gave him a once over. Jeff looked dapper in a white T-shirt and jeans. He'd always had a knack as a trend setter of sorts with fashion.

"Aren't you even a little bit happy to see me?"

Happy to see him? She wondered how he found

the courage to ask that question. The last time she'd had an encounter with him, he had left her feeling more humiliated than she'd ever felt in her life. Not before, not since.

"Well?" Jeff asked. He looked directly into her eyes.

Carrie met his gaze, but remained silent. Why in the world, after all this time, had he sought her out?

"It's good to see you, Carrie. I've missed you." His eyebrows pulled together. "I miss you."

"If you recall, it was your choice to walk away from the relationship."

He nodded. "I know. And I regret that."

"Jeff, it has been two years since our breakup…"

He threw up a hand. "I know. And it's been a miserable two years for me."

"Well, that's too bad. I have moved on."

"Does saying I'm sorry not mean anything to you?"

"No. Not now."

"No forgiveness in your heart?" He arched a pathetic brow.

"I forgave you a long time ago." But the hurt took much longer to recoup from, she thought. That had lasted many months.

"You were the best thing in my life."

"You sure didn't act like our life together meant anything to you."

"I know I acted like a heel."

"Yes, you did."

"I am so sorry I hurt you." He angled his head, his eyes locked on hers. "I'm not ready to let what we had slip away."

Carrie sighed and shifted in her chair. She hadn't let herself remember that time in her life for a long time, but now while she listened to Jeff's words, she felt herself drift back.

For months after Jeff broke up with her, she wouldn't let him go, imagining scenarios she might use to win him back. They had started dating in high school and she never had another boyfriend. Jeff was enough. She'd loved him with her whole heart and soul. And she felt certain he'd reciprocated her love. He'd even asked her to marry him, but she was the one who said they needed to wait, so they both decided to see other people while they were in college. Her four years at University of Tampa were a blur of busyness and activities, led by her involvement with the school newspaper and drama department. Not much time for dating other people. Not that she wanted to. Jeff had always been enough. When he pulled back, she held on with all her might. When he told her he'd found someone else, she'd begged him to not leave her. She spent months grieving his loss. Now he wanted to resume where they'd left off?

"It slipped away a long time ago."

"Aww, Carrie. . ." Long horizontal lines creased his forehead.

Carrie shook her head, disgusted. She looked at her watch. "I've got to get back to work in five minutes. Was there anything else you wanted to talk about?" She watched Jeff's face cloud with uncertainty. He wasn't used to her not giving in to him.

"I'd hoped for a little more time to talk, but since

that's a bust, I'll just get right to it." He rubbed his chin. "The other woman, the one I let ruin things between you and me, well she dumped me. I guess I deserved it. But it made me realize it was you I wanted all along."

If she'd heard these words several months ago, things could've been different. She wouldn't have hesitated for one second to take him back. And though she could still feel a twinge of emotion toward him, she would never allow herself to fall for his laudatory words again.

Before she could form a reply, Jeff scooted his chair close to hers, laid an arm across her shoulder, drew her close, then kissed her, a kiss that lingered too long. Surprised, it took several beats for Carrie to pull back. When she managed to push him back, he was still so close she could see the faint flecks of gold in his eyes, which made the dark brown look that much darker. She lowered her gaze, but that meant she was looking at his mouth. The familiarity of his lips stirred memories. However, the kiss did not shoot sparks throughout her body. Not like Kent's did. And she knew, once and for all, no doubt about it. She was completely free from a past with Jeff. Her future was with Kent.

Fury burned through Carrie. He was way out of bounds with his actions and she wouldn't put up with it. She placed both hands on Jeff's chest, pushing him back. "Don't do that again." She stood, walked away from him and from a past that had haunted her for two long years.

* * *

Kent took the elevator to the fourth floor and walked to the nurse's counter. No Carrie in sight. He peered down the hall, hoping to catch a glimpse of her.

"If you're looking for Carrie, she's in the cafeteria." Brenda laughed and tossed him a knowing look. "You better hurry. She's been gone half an hour."

"Thanks." Kent gave her a two-finger salute, then headed down the hall.

He raced to the cafeteria because he didn't want to miss Carrie. Even if for just a few minutes.

Kent's steps slowed, then came to an abrupt halt when he spotted Carrie kissing some man. And right there in the cafeteria. All the eagerness to see her drained from his heart, and he turned on his heel and headed out of the lunch room. He sure didn't feel hungry any more.

Back in his office, he opened a drawer and took out a power bar. What a fool he'd been. The amount of time he'd spent dreaming about Carrie far exceeded the amount of time they'd actually spent together. But their time together had been the most memorable hours of his entire life. Obviously, it had not meant that much to Carrie. How could he have read her so wrong?

It was time to get to work, forget the encounter he'd witnessed. He opened his PC and clicked to emails. He replied to a few, but soon grew restless.

He scooted back from his desk and walked to the window. The sun filtering through the pane felt warm on his face. He leaned his forehead against the window, totally confused. He hated that he'd allowed himself to be so taken in by Carrie's sweet persona.

A blue jay perched on the windowsill. Its head bobbed while it pecked at something Kent couldn't quite make out. Growing tired of its labor, the bird flew away. Like Kent wanted to do.

CHAPTER TWENTY-THREE

When Kent woke up Saturday morning he felt like he hadn't slept a wink. He'd tossed and turned all night, just dozing on and off. Every time he woke up, visions of Carrie in another man's arms flooded his mind, making him nauseous.

At six AM he gave up any thoughts of sleep and dragged his worn-out body into the shower, which usually relaxed him. But not today. Today the familiar routine did nothing to calm him. He toweled off in the bathroom, reviewing the long, crummy night he'd had. Something told him every night from here on out would fit that description.

He raked a hand through his wet hair and slipped into a T-shirt and shorts. He'd felt so good about the direction he and Carrie were headed. How could he have misread her? Had he just imagined things between them were progressing smoothly? His mind flashed on how her lips had felt when they had kissed. He couldn't have imagined that. Then he chided himself for being so naïve about someone he hardly knew. Someone he'd allowed into to his heart like he'd never allowed another woman to do. Ever.

Driven to get some air, he walked to the front door and opened it. He hadn't been to the marsh behind his complex yet, and it was closer than the beach. He left the apartment and strolled down the sidewalk. Behind the complex was a well-worn path that circled through underbrush, and he made his way through the scrub pines. Needles pricked his forearms but he forged on.

Humidity weighed heavy in the air, making his shirt cling to his chest. He reached the clearing and took in the view of the water. Sun shimmered on the surface, making shifting shadows of darkness and light. Ducks flapped their wings while they landed. The mosquitoes and horseflies buzzed around his head. He inhaled, but it smelled like decomposing things. He huffed. Just like his life.

The sudden thoughts of walking on the Tampa Riverwalk hand in hand with Carrie overtook him. He'd felt certain something special had developed between them. Had he been so out of tune with Carrie he'd fooled himself into believing he could actually have a future with her?

He ran a hand over his face and his prickly jaw reminded him he hadn't shaved. Who cared? he thought. Nobody would be touching his face anytime soon.

After walking to edge of the marsh, his cell alerted him to an incoming call.

His pulled the phone from his pocket and looked at Carrie's smiling face on the screen. He rubbed his brow and pondered his options before he decided he would take the call. What the heck, he thought. He'd listen to what she had to say.

"Hello."

"Hey, Kent."

He remained silent. He'd let her say what she'd called to say.

"Are you okay?"

"Me? I'm fine. Why do you ask?"

"You sound different. . ."

"Oh?"

"Maybe we have a bad connection."

"Carrie, I can hear you just fine."

"Oh, okay. I just called to tell you Dad got the biopsy results."

"Good news, I hope." Kent cared about Carrie's father and had prayed for benign results. He'd prayed for Carrie and her family too.

"Yes. Great news. The results are negative."

He could hear the smile in her voice and for a split second felt everything was okay between them.

"I'm glad. I know how upset and concerned you were."

"Thank you. And thank you for your prayers."

"No problem."

"He has an appointment with the oncologist next week to discuss what follow-up they will do. If any. I'm hoping for the not any."

"Yes, that would be the best news."

"Well. . ." Carrie hesitated then cleared her throat and added, "That's all I wanted. I guess I'll let you go."

"Okay. Take it easy."

* * *

Take it easy? What did that mean? Carrie's mind ran full speed. Why had he seemed so distant with her? He'd never treated her like that before. It was obvious he'd blown her off. Maybe she'd called him at an inopportune time, catching him off guard. It didn't matter what it was, his attitude busted her bubble, diluting the excitement she'd felt about Dad's good news.

Memories of Jeff pulling back from their relationship gnawed at her gut. At first she'd blown of his lackadaisical attitude toward her. She wouldn't let herself believe anything was wrong between them. Even when he'd announced he had someone else, she'd not accepted it. She'd told herself it was just a phase; he'd come to his senses and come back to her. How simple-minded she'd been. Or just plain stupid, she thought. Tears stung her eyes, and she swiped them away.

She laid down the cell phone and stepped into her kitchen. Keeping her emotions under tight control, she managed not to burst out in frantic tears.

Could this be history repeating itself? Had she been manipulated yet again?

She replayed the last time she'd spent with Kent. What had they discussed? The questions spun round and round in her head. Surely she hadn't said something that had scared him off. Maybe her initiative in kissing him was a turn-off. Some men like to be the one to make the first move. Be the one in charge. Her blood pulsed hot and fast. If that was the kind of man he was, then so be it. She'd felt heartsick, sad, and more than a little frightened about Dad's diagnosis, so she'd reached out to Kent. She'd needed to be held and comforted. At the time, she'd thought Kent was okay with her sudden move.

Her phone buzzed, popping her back to the present. Please be Kent, she told the cell, but when she checked the text, it was Brenda. *Call me when you're free to talk.*

Carrie pulled in a breath. She hoped her supervisor didn't want her to come in to work. She was not in the mood. She tapped Brenda's memory button.

"Hey, Carrie. I didn't want to bother you on your day off. . ."

"No problem." Carrie blew out a relieved breath. "Is there an issue at work?" Carrie knew things in the unit could change in a heartbeat, from increased admissions to decreased staff.

"No. Everything's fine here."

"Okay. What's going on then?"

"There's something I wanted to tell you with no one around. I'm sure what I'm going to say will upset you."

Carrie felt a chill race up her spine. "Brenda, you are starting to scare me."

"Sorry, didn't mean to do that."

"Just out with it. What do you want to tell me?"

"It's about Kent."

"What about him?"

"I had to go to the admin office to pick up some new specs. . ."

Carrie pushed a strand of hair behind her ear. She wished Brenda would spit out whatever was on her mind. "And?"

"And I walked in on a scene I wished I'd never witnessed."

"I have a feeling this isn't good news."

"No, it isn't. Kent's door was ajar, and just as I was about to enter, I saw Kent with a knockout of a woman in his clutches."

Carrie sucked in air, but fell silent.

"I backed out pronto and confronted Sheila. His secretary admitted the woman was a frequent flyer and had visited him on more than one occasion."

"Ahh." Carrie shook her head. That explained everything. Kent hadn't been serious about her at all. What a player. Why did she always attract the users? "Thank you for filling me in while I'm home. I would not want to hear this kind of news with a unit full of people to witness me falling apart."

"I am so sorry, Carrie. You don't deserve what he did to you."

Carrie felt tears fall from her eyes, felt her world collapse. She'd been such a fool to trust a man again. Would she ever learn?

"Do you want me to come over after work?"

"No. Just let me wallow in self-pity alone." She tried to laugh to cover her broken heart. "I'll cry, get it out of my system, then I'll be okay."

"Are you sure?"

"I'm sure."

"Okay then, I will see you Monday."

"Remember, I won't be in until noon. I'm meeting Dad at the cancer center. He has a consult with the oncologist Monday morning."

"Okay. I'll say a prayer."

* * *

She gathered her PC, plopped in the recliner and face-timed her sisters.

"Hey Boo Boo." Abby leaned closer to the screen. "Are you okay?"

"I'm terrible." Carrie couldn't stop the tears that leaked from her eyes. "Even worse than terrible."

"Oh, sweetie, tell us what's happened," Abby said.

"Kent." She sniffed, then blew her nose.

"What about Kent?" Emily's eyes grew round. "Is he okay? Did he have an accident?"

"He's just fine." Carrie bit her lower lip. "But I'm not."

"You aren't making a whole lot of sense." Abby scratched her head. "Come on Carrie, tell us what's happened."

"He's dumped me."

"No way." Disbelief flooded Abby's face.

Carrie blew her nose again and shrugged her shoulders and fell silent.

"That doesn't sound like him." Emmy tapped her chin.

"Sure doesn't," Abby agreed. "Sam said the

Saturday he'd spent with Kent, he could tell how much Kent was in to you."

"You know, I thought that too." Carrie bit her lower lip. "I really thought he loved me. I guess he fooled all of us."

"Did you two have a fight?" Emily's brow shot up.

"No. No fight." Carrie dabbed her eyes with a tissue. "Brenda walked in on him making out with some woman."

"You have got to be kidding." Abby shook her head. "I'd never figure he'd do something like that."

Carrie nodded. "When Brenda questioned Sheila, his secretary, she told Brenda that the woman had made several visits to Kent's office."

Abby made a heart shape with her hands, held them to the screen. "I'm speechless."

"Ditto," Emmy agreed. "I can only imagine how hard the news hit you."

"Hurt to the core. Tore my heart out."

Family had been important in the home she'd grown up in, so it was no surprise her two older sisters were always willing to stand by her, ready and willing to help her. She adored her sisters and always strived to be just like them. Growing up, her siblings had left her with big shoes to fill. And after spending most of her childhood trying to keep up with her sisters, her competitive streak was well-honed.

"Makes me a two-time loser, huh?"

"Don't say that. This is not your fault." Abby pulled her hair back. "But maybe there's an explanation to all this. Have you talked to him about it?"

Carrie laughed. "What kind of explanation would justify what he's pulled?"

"Remember you told us how Jeff cornered you in the cafeteria and ended up grabbing you and kissing you?" Abby waved her hand in the air. "You said it happened so fast it took you a minute before you gained your thoughts enough to push him away."

Carrie nodded.

Abby continued, "Well, maybe, just maybe, something similar happened with Kent."

"Think about it, Carrie," Emily said. "All of this is so out of character for Kent. It doesn't ring true somehow. I think you need to give him the benefit of the doubt. Don't judge until you hear the facts from his mouth."

"I do not see how talking to him would make any difference." Carrie remembered when she'd had the heart to heart talk with Jeff. She'd left that visit even more hurt and completely humiliated.

"Humor us. Give him a chance to explain about the woman." Abby made prayer hands. "Please, for us?"

Carrie blew out a breath. "Okay. I will talk to him. For you guys. So you will get off my back. And when it doesn't do one bit of good, at least I would have given it the good ole college try." She tried to laugh, but it didn't sound convincing, not even to her.

Emily pointed a finger at the screen. "You owe it to yourself to hear first-hand what's going on with him."

"Okay, already. I said I'd talk to him."

CHAPTER TWENTY-FOUR

Monday morning, Carrie dressed quickly, choosing a lightweight calf-length floral print dress. She had extra scrubs in her locker at the hospital for a fast change later in the afternoon.

Adding a touch of makeup, she was ready to meet her parents at the cancer center.

Traffic was light and she arrived at the clinic before them. She slipped her phone from her purse, touched the screen to wake it up, and checked her messages. She had two texts, one from each sibling, asking for reports of Dad's visit ASAP. She replied with a thumbs up.

A tap on her window caused her to look up. It was Dad.

She tucked her phone away, opened her door, then stepped out.

"Are you ready to hear the news?" Dad's brows pulled together.

"Yes. I'm ready." Expecting a positive report, Carrie linked arms with her parents. "More than ready to hear the good news."

"From your lips, to God's ears." Mom's mouth quivered.

They walked into the Cancer Center, signed in, then were ushered to the exam room in record time.

Carrie held her mother's hand during Dad's thorough exam.

After the examination, the Oncologist reviewed her father's file on his iPad, then scooted his stool so he could face Dad, Mom and her.

"From what I've seen today and what is in your file, I don't feel there is a need for any further treatment at this time." The corners of the doctor's eyes crinkled when he smiled. "Looks like you are good to go, but I'd like to see you again in three months."

Carrie pulled in a relieved breath and a ripple of excitement ran up her spine. No chemo.

Her dad's grin split his genial face and he said, "Thanks, doc."

"And if you should have any questions or concerns, please give us a call." The doctor extended his smooth hand and patted Dad's shoulder. Then he walked out the door.

After the three-month appointment had been made, Dad turned and Carrie could see the relief in his eyes.

"I'm springing for lunch, again," he said.

Carrie nodded and stepped outside into a

beautiful April day that lacked the usual Florida humidity. Relieved for the good report, she whispered a silent thank-you prayer. At least she had one thing she could be thankful for.

"Where to? Your choice." Dad's mouth grew a smile. "You deserve the best. Thanks for standing by me. You can't know how much I appreciate your support, Carrie girl."

"You've always stood by me."

"Yeah, but that's my job."

"Ya think?"

"I know."

"Okay, you guys. Enough with the compliments." Mom chuckled.

Her mother's laughter sounded like music to Carrie's ears. If something bad ever happened to her dad, her mother would be devastated.

"I don't have to be at work until one o'clock, so let's skip the fast-food places and splurge today. Eat somewhere nice."

"Name the place." Dad tossed her an agreeable wink.

"Bahama Breeze." Located on the water, Carrie loved their food and great atmosphere.

"Sounds good," Mom said.

"Headed that way." Dad gave her a thumbs up. "And I'm starved."

"Me too," Mom said.

After her father found a parking space, Carrie shaded her eyes with her hand as the three of them walked beside the pier. The early noon-time sun glinted off the waves, reminding her of Kent. She sucked in a breath. Everything reminded her of

Kent. She doubted she'd ever accomplish the feat of not thinking about him. A pelican tipped its head to gawk at her, then flapped off on big wings. Lucky bird, she thought. She wished she could fly away to a happier time.

"Are you coming?" Dad's words pulled Carrie back to the here and now.

"Sorry, Dad, my mind wandered." Carrie stepped through the doorway while Dad held it open for her and Mom.

After the hostess greeted them and guided them to a table that faced the Gulf, the waiter appeared and took their drink orders. He returned in record time with three large glasses of sweet tea.

"Ready to order?" The good-looking young man aimed a pen at his pad.

"Could we have the Crab and Three Cheese Dip to start?" Dad asked.

Carrie smiled. Her father knew she loved the dip. A quarter pound of crab in creamy cheeses, served hot in a skillet with tortilla chips and lime always pleased her.

Carrie listened while Dad ordered a Honey Butter Crispy Chicken Sandwich, and Mom nodded and said she wanted the same.

"I'll have the Coconut Shrimp Tacos." Carrie could never resist something that contained coconut.

"Your order will be right out." The waiter tucked the pen in his shirt pocket then walked away.

Carrie glanced out the window that butted up to the side of their table and studied the timeless, gentle motion of the blue-green Caribbean water.

She loved everything about the ocean, especially the gulf side. So calm. It was hypnotizing.

"You seem down today, honey." Mom furrowed her brow. "What's wrong?"

Carrie picked up her glass and took a sip of tea. She had scolded Dad for not keeping her updated. She decided she owed her parents the same consideration.

"Things didn't work out between Kent and me."

Mom gave her a startled look. "Oh my. I never saw that coming."

"Me neither." Tears burned Carrie's eyes and she blinked them back. She didn't want to spoil Dad's good news with a crying session. She knew how he worried about his daughters.

"So what happened?" Mom shook her head.

"I guess he has someone else."

The waiter stepped to the table with the appetizer and placed it in the middle of the table. He positioned three small plates beside the steaming dip before he left.

"Someone else? How'd that happen?" Dad's voice shot up an octave. "Who is she?"

Carrie shrugged. "Beats me."

"How do you know it's true?" Dad massaged his forehead with his fingertips. "Seeing you and Kent together, watching how you two interact with each other, well I guess I just thought Kent would never do something like that."

"The truth is, Brenda saw him and another woman kissing in his office."

"If that don't beat all. . ." Dad's startled voice trailed off and he released a heavy sigh.

"I never thought he'd pull something like that either. He sure seemed different than Jeff." Mom raised an eyebrow. "I had such a good feeling about him too."

"He hoodwinked all of us." Dad reached for a tortilla chip and raked it through the creamy dip.

Carrie filled a small plate with the crab dip, fisted some tortillas, and placed them to the side, then picked one up and spread it generously with the dip. She sank her teeth into the wedge and the first bite burst with flavor. Hot, creamy and spicy. She chewed and swallowed.

Before she finished the second tortilla, the waiter brought the entrees and placed them accordingly.

"I am genuinely sorry, Carrie." Mom picked up her sandwich. "The last thing I wanted to see is you getting your heart broken again."

Too late, Carrie thought, but she held her tongue. "Abby and Emmy said I need to talk to him. Confront him with what Brenda saw."

"You know that's a good idea," Mom said. "Could be there is a logical explanation."

Carrie threw her hands in the air. "How can kissing someone in the privacy of your office have any other explanation other than what it appears to be?"

"You're probably right." Dad pinched the bridge of his nose. "It sounds pretty suspicious for sure."

Mom cleared her throat. "Don't judge until you know all the facts."

Dad harrumphed and the skin between his eyebrows formed wrinkles. "I'd like to sit down and have a little talk with that man myself."

"Now, now, don't get yourself all upset. Let your daughter take care of it."

Carrie nodded. "Mom's right. I'll deal with him. I promised my sisters I'd talk to him. So I guess I'll have to do it."

"They will keep after you until you comply." Dad picked up his sandwich and held it mid-air. "You know that for a fact."

"Oh, yes." Carrie laughed "How well I know."

Carrie took a deep breath. She realized that her siblings were right. She needed to talk to Kent in order to move forward with her own life.

CHAPTER TWENTY-FIVE

Reviewing the long crummy day he'd spent yesterday, Kent stepped from the shower and grabbed a towel. Something told him his lousy days were far from over. He'd felt lost since he'd seen Carrie with the man in the cafeteria. The revelation of spending more days alone, without Carrie's uplifting spirit, caused his chest to tighten.

He dressed and went into the kitchen. After a bowl of cornflakes with a ripe banana sliced on top, orange juice, and two cups of very strong coffee, he headed to his jeep.

After driving to the hospital, he found a parking spot, and headed to his office. He couldn't shake the sight of Carrie and the man kissing in the cafeteria. So obvious. She hadn't even tried to be discreet about it. He would have thought she'd have shown more professionalism.

"Good morning, Kent." His secretary smiled. "How was your weekend?"

"Probably not as good as yours, Sheila." He tried to make his voice sound a lot more upbeat than he felt.

"You want to bet? I spent two days nursing my puppy back to health. He had a frightful stomach bug. Poor baby, he vomited non-stop Saturday."

"Bummer. I am truly sorry. Hope he's better."

"He is. The Vet gave me an antiemetic for him. He felt lots better Sunday."

"Good." Kent turned on his heel, walked through his office doorway, seated himself behind the desk and opened his computer. After he entered his passcode he shuffled through his emails, deleting the ones he'd already addressed.

Sheila came in with a detailed list of the day's appointments. He was thankful for his secretary. She was smart and efficient. No drama with her. Not like with other women in his life, he thought.

He had a conference call scheduled at 10 AM with the hospital association and other CEOs to discuss their collaborated response to proposed reimbursement reductions. Last week they'd decided to form a committee to address this issue, so today would be the day.

After that, he would make an impromptu walk-through in the ED and Cardiac Critical Care unit, just to support the staff and ensure things were running smoothly. He sighed, remembering the intimate lunch he'd shared with Carrie after his last visit with the departments.

Someone cleared their throat.

He turned around. Ellen stood in the doorway, a sly smile spreading across her face. He had to admit, she was a good-looking woman. But not a woman he wanted to deal with. Especially not now.

"Hey, lover." Ellen kicked the door shut behind her with her foot. "Miss me?" She paced to his desk and plopped both hands flat on the surface.

Kent scooted his chair back, stood and walked to the door, then pulled it open. He wasn't taking any more chances with her.

"Scared to be in a closed room with me?" Ellen's eyebrows bounced up and down.

"No, not scared." Kent spread his hands. "Just being careful."

"Why now?"

"Why now, what?"

"Why be sensible now?"

"Come on Ellen, don't start talking nonsense again."

Ellen plopped down in the chair situated in front of his desk. When she crossed her arms around her chest he knew she meant business. He'd better get her out of here fast.

"Why are you being so dang mean to me? All I ever did was love you."

"Please don't go there. I've told you how I feel and where we stand. There never was anything but friendship between us. And you've even ruined that."

"How, pray tell, did I ruin it?" Ellen pushed her lower lip forward in her characteristic pout.

"I don't have time for this. It's useless to spend

endless minutes going over what's already been said and repeated numerous times." He motioned toward the door. "Now it's time for you to leave. And don't make a scene."

"Oh, I can make a scene all right." Ellen waved her hand through the air as though she were chasing off a fly. "You know how good I am at that."

Arctic air settled in his chest and a fist of fear wrapped its cold fingers around his rib cage. Yes, he did know how good she was at throwing fits. And causing trouble ran a close second.

Kent fell silent, reaching for the right words to say. Words that would convince her to not only leave his office, but also leave his life.

Ellen stood and ran a rigid hand down the side of her pants. "Okay, I'm out of here. For now. But I'll be back and we'll continue our nice long talk, lover." She narrowed her eyes. "You can count on it."

Pulling in a deep cleansing breath, Kent watched her strut out of his office. The air somehow felt sweeter once she'd exited the room, as if a lurking evil had taken off for parts unknown, leaving him to breathe easy again. Oh how he regretted the day he'd met her.

CHAPTER TWENTY-SIX

When Carrie entered the Trauma Surgery Unit the following day, she felt like she'd swallowed a ball of lead. And with every step she took in the direction of the nurse's station, the sensation intensified as if the ball was expanding and taking more and more room in her gut.

She hadn't been this upset since the unbearable breakup with Jeff two years ago. The call from Brenda on Saturday had landed on her full force, ripping through her like a Florida hurricane. She would have preferred to ride out a windstorm.

The heaviness in the bottom of her stomach had nothing to do with the sleepless night she'd just spent. Or did it?

She'd laid in bed awake most of the night replaying the information she'd learned about Kent.

The last thing she'd wanted to do was fret about him. And as much as she had refused to waste a second of her time crying over him, she had. Which was ridiculous, because why would she want to allow him to take space in her head? Obviously, he wouldn't give her a second thought.

She and Kent hadn't made a commitment and didn't owe each other anything. And the way he'd smiled at her, and whatever he'd said to her, should have bounced right off of her. It was her own fault for falling for his charm and allowing him to deceive her.

She shook off all of Kent's drama and buried the kernel of uneasiness so it couldn't continue to grow into something larger and more hurtful.

Being the first to arrive, she slipped behind the nursing counter, opened her planner and shuffled through a few reminders she'd jotted down. She felt a soft brush of a hand on her arm, and the light scent of lemon. She turned, already knowing who she'd find smiling down at her.

"Hey, where to for lunch?" Brenda asked.

"I'd give a crisp fifty-dollar bill for a greasy burger and a side of fries. But I shouldn't."

"Why not?"

"I ate way too much at Bahama Breeze yesterday. But I had to celebrate Dad's good news."

"Well today you need to celebrate the news with your friend."

Carrie chuckled, and before she could answer, her stomach grumbled. "Kinda regretting I skipped breakfast."

"Let's do Butlers Burgers." Brenda's eyes

narrowed, and she gave Carrie a look that said she wouldn't be put off.

"Trust me, after the night I had, I'd be happy to let you whisk me away, but it's gonna be no."

"You skipped breakfast." Brenda arched an eyebrow, searched Carrie's face, and apparently found something there. "I'm not going to let you skip lunch. You need to talk to me, let me know what's going on in that little head of yours."

Carrie placed flat palms on the counter, a little huff leaving her lips. "I'll tell you later."

Her friend's eyes filled with concern. "At Butlers?"

"Okay. You win. Butlers." Her mood would plummet down even more if she isolated herself. And she, for sure, wanted to avoid the hospital cafeteria and any chance she might run into Kent.

Then suddenly her Kent radar went off. The woodsy hint of lime scent wafted over her, warning her of his presence. It caught her completely off guard.

Her heart lurched in her chest, and her gaze hunted him down. The organ under her rib cage sped up when Kent turned and looked toward her, his eyes meeting hers across the unit. She noticed she focused on him a little too intensely for someone who had sworn she wouldn't let him get to her. Never again.

Her cheeks flushed hot and it felt like her face was on fire. And yet, she couldn't avert her eyes from his. It was Kent who looked away, ignoring her. His message rang out loud and clear. He had no use for her. Not anymore because he'd found someone else. And he wasn't even man enough to tell her.

That hurt. Something about the fact that he had just dismissed her so quickly cut to the core.

For an instant, she was hurled back in time. To a past she'd left behind and did not want to remember. Was this a replay of Jeff's kiss-off? Shaking her head, she tried to erase the whirlwind of unwelcome memories that flooded her mind.

Her gaze, which still latched like a magnet on Kent, watched him walk away from her. Just like that, everything changed. Whatever she'd imagined was between them floated away, like dust in a windstorm. Nothing he'd intimated to her mattered because, now she was through being played the fool. Not by him. Not by any other man. There was no way she'd ever put herself in a situation to be hurt again.

She'd been right. He'd obviously gone back to whatever he did before he met her. He'd probably had the girlfriend all along. She wondered how the other woman would feel if she knew he'd spent time with Carrie? In her arms?

She tried to be strong but tears filled her eyes, then spilled over. She headed to the restroom, and pushed through the doorway, with Brenda on her heels.

Brenda yanked tissues from the container on the counter and handed them to her.

"He blew me off big time." Carrie swiped at her eyes, blew her nose. "Did you see how obvious he was?"

"I am so sorry."

"Why do I always pick guys that end up hurting me?" Carrie snuffled and blew her nose.

Brenda gathered her in her arms. "Let it out. Let it all out."

"Imagine if you spent all your high school and college years in love with one guy. Faithful to him from day one. Then only when he dumps you, you realize you meant nothing to him." Carrie sobbed until a a bout of uncontrollable hiccupping took her breath.

A few short minutes later she gulped down the water Brenda handed her in a paper cup, then wiped her face with a paper towel.

"Thanks for letting me use your shoulder as a crying post."

"What are friends for?"

"Not all friends are as supportive as you." She gave her friend a long hug. "Again, thank you so much."

"It's lunch time. Let's head out of here. It will do you good to get away from the hospital for a while. Clear your head."

Carrie nodded and wiped her eyes. "I'm in." She loved where she worked and felt extremely blessed to have a job she looked forward to every day. However, getting away from Tampa General for an hour suddenly sounded perfect.

* * *

Kent strode to the elevator on the Trauma Surgery Unit. He had to put distance between him and Carrie. When he'd seen her, the familiar feelings of excitement and love had seeped through his veins. He'd wanted to talk to her, confront her about what he'd witnessed in the lunchroom. Ask her why she'd even considered kissing someone in the middle of the hospital cafeteria. But even if he thought it would do any good, the hospital was not the place to take care of personal problems. Especially for the CEO. When, and if, he talked to her, it would be off site. Somewhere private.

When he'd noticed her looking at him, his heart melted. Those beautiful brown eyes always worked magic on his soul. Or they had at one time. Before he'd seen her wrapped in that guy's arms. The memory of her sitting there, lip locked with a strange man in the middle of the cafeteria caused knots to form in his gut. He'd been so sure she felt the same sparks he'd felt when they were together. He sighed. He guessed he'd just been fooling himself.

After he exited the elevator on the administrative floor, he made a bee-line to his office, nodding to Sheila as he passed her workspace. Then he stepped through the doorway and fell into his desk chair. He placed his elbows on the desktop and dropped his head into his hands. He wanted to cry, but couldn't. He figured if he could have a good cry, he'd feel better. But the tears stayed hidden behind his eyes. But, for sure, his heart wept. He could feel the tears dripping steady and sure from that organ.

His cell rang, and he pulled it from his pocket. It was Ellen again. He rubbed tired eyes, then declined the call. She was quickly becoming a borderline stalker and he'd had it with her. He opened his PC and documented the time the call was made. He decided to keep notes of her calls and visits.

The rest of the day inched by. Though he remained busy, he couldn't shake the look he'd seen in Carrie's eyes. His stomach felt like he'd taken a gut punch. He felt as though he was swimming in the ocean with no land in sight. By the time he'd locked his office door at six, he'd worked himself into a class-A mess.

He realized he'd have to release his anxiety, forget about Carrie, and get on with his life, hard as that seemed. But right now, in the present moment, she filled his every thought.

"Have a good night," he said to Sheila. "Be sure and lock up when you leave." Sheila usually stayed until he headed out, then she would tidy up the waiting area before she left for the evening.

"You too."

He started to leave, but when she called his name, he turned. "Yes?"

"I know this is none of my business. . ."

Kent looked at his secretary. "Is something wrong?"

"Well, I don't know." She shifted her weight from one foot to the other. "That woman. You know the one that's been here a few times?"

"What about her?" Good grief, he thought, he didn't need this drama from Sheila. Not now.

"She came by again today when you were out. I think you'd gone to lunch, not sure though."

"I do not want to see her." Kent spoke in a slow contained whisper, sliding the words through his lips tight with fury. "If she comes here again, please tell her I'm not in. I hate asking you to lie, but she is stalking me."

Sheila's jaw dropped. "I had no idea. I'm so sorry."

"So, what did she say today?"

"She spent fifteen minutes telling me about your time with her in Kansas City. She said you were going to have her move in with you."

"We are not a couple. Never have been." Kent felt a blade of rage slice his spine. "I dated her a few times in Kansas City, that's it. She acts like she's obsessed with me and will not leave me alone. And I did not ask her to move in with me."

Sheila shook her head, a stunned look slid across her face.

"I've changed my mind. If she comes back, don't lie to her. Just step in my office and let me know she's here. I will call security. I am not going to put up with her nonsense any more. If I'm not careful, she'll cause me trouble."

"I think she already has."

"How? What do you mean?"

"Well, last week Brenda, the Trauma Surgery Unit Supervisor, came to see you. Ellen was in the office with you, so Brenda didn't go in. Before she left she asked me a lot of questions about who the woman was. She asked how many times she'd been here to see you. The more I answered her questions, the angrier she became. When I asked her why she was so upset, she said because when she started to go into your office, she stopped because you and the woman were kissing. She muttered something about you treating her friend like a heel, then stomped out."

"Oh my." Kent ran a hand through his hair. Maybe that's why Carrie allowed that guy to kiss her in the cafeteria. If she thought I was fooling around behind her back, she probably set out to get revenge. But getting revenge didn't fit Carrie. He couldn't blow off her actions using that excuse. "It's a long story, Sheila. I'll fill you in later."

* * *

Somehow Carrie made it through lunch at Butlers Burgers without succumbing to another cry fest. She even managed to have a semi-calm conversation with Brenda while she picked at the greasy food.

Later when Carrie took her afternoon break, she inserted coins into the vending machine in the breakroom, punched the corresponding button for a peanut butter power bar, and waited until it was dispensed. Then she filled a Styrofoam cup with coffee from a machine that was available 24/7 for the staff.

After she took a seat, she opened the snack and took a bite. She sent texts to her siblings, updating them on her day.

Just when she started to slip her phone into her pocket, the cell rang. It was Sara.

"Hey, graduation girl. How's it going now that you don't have to hit the books non-stop?"

"Feels kinda odd, having so much free time."

Carrie laughed. "Oh, you'll adjust."

"Doesn't seem possible I'm done with college. I

can't believe it. The three years went fast. But I'm ready to rock-n-roll now."

"You go, girlfriend." Carrie smiled. Sara's enthusiasm reminded her so much of herself when she'd graduated college. Ready to tackle the world.

"What's your schedule looking like next week?"

"My days off will be Tuesday and Wednesday. Why?"

"I'm thinking you and I need to go do something fun."

"Oh yeah?" Carrie valued the friendship she had with Sam's oldest daughter. Sara had felt uncertain about the future when she'd moved in with her dad and Abby. Since Carrie and Sara were close in age, they'd formed an immediate bond, and it had lasted through time.

"Yeah."

"What exactly do you think we need to do?"

"Disney World. I haven't been there in forever."

"You know, that sounds good to me. I haven't been in quite a while either."

"We could head to Orlando early Tuesday morning and have all day at Disney. Spend the night and then have another full day on Wednesday before we head home."

"It's a date."

"Okay, I'll pick you up at your place on Monday after you get home from work."

"See you then."

After they said their goodbyes, Carrie shut her phone and smiled. She'd needed a boost to lift her spirits, and Sara had brought a glimmer of sunshine to her life just when she needed it. Even if it was only for a minute.

Carrie finished the power bar and downed the remains of her sweet tea. She had five minutes left of her break. She slipped her phone into her pocket.

The afternoon passed without her running into Kent again. She wasn't sure her fragile heart could have handled another encounter. Her mood remained overcast by the storm clouds that hovered above her head whenever Kent came to mind.

CHAPTER TWENTY-SEVEN

Carrie opened the door Tuesday morning to Sara's flushed face.

"I know I'm a little early." Sara's eyes grew round. "Are you ready to hit the road?"

"Absolutely." Carrie smiled. She could hear the excitement in Sara's voice.

She trailed Sara to her car, tossed her overnight bag in the back, then slipped into the passenger seat. She was more than ready to get away from Tampa for a couple days.

"Disney, here we come," Sara said.

"Let's swing through Scooters and get a coffee." Carrie loved their Candy Bar Latte.

"Sounds good."

In less than ten minutes, when Sara turned into the parking lot, Carrie noticed the drive-through line was three cars deep.

"This place is always busy," Carrie said. "Especially on weekends."

"It won't take long to get through the line." Sara pulled behind a Jeep.

Carrie jerked forward and sucked in an audible breath. "Oh no."

"What?"

"That's Kent." Carrie pointed to the car in front of them.

"Oh, wow. Who would have thought?" Sara's eyebrows drew together. "At least he's alone. That's a good sign. Saturday. Alone."

"It's early. So that means absolutely nothing."

"You wish it did though, don't you?"

"It doesn't matter what I wish. What is, is."

"Never give up on your dreams, Carrie."

Carrie chuckled. Who was this person giving such sage advice?

The line moved swiftly, and before Carrie knew it, Sara's car pulled up to the window and Kent drove away. She wondered if he'd even seen her. Most likely he wouldn't have recognized Sara's car.

Drinks in tow, they left the coffee shop behind, hit I-4 and were on their hour and a half drive to Disney World.

"So Carrie, did you ever figure out who Kent is involved with?"

"No. I have no idea." She took a careful sip from her hot beverage. "Haven't a clue where she came from."

"Did you ever talk to him about it?"

"Not yet."

"Carrie!"

She shrugged. "Sorry."

"And why not?"

"I don't know. I haven't found the right opportunity yet I guess."

"Listen Boo Boo, you've got to make the opportunity happen."

Carrie tossed Sara a fake frown, but laughed. She'd never be able to shake off that silly nickname. "I know. I promised Abby and Emily I'd talk to him even though I doubt it will change anything. So don't worry, I will."

Carrie recognized the look Sara gave her. Her niece's expression made it seem like she had more to say, but Carrie didn't press her. No need to continue a conversation about Kent. Her past.

"What about you, Sara? Are you dating anyone seriously?"

"Naw." Sara's brows bounced up and down. "I'm going out occasionally with Ben. I met him at U of T. But I emphasize occasionally."

"Why just occasionally?"

"He's nice and all. But I'm just not that into him."

"I see." Carrie repressed a chuckle. She'd noticed a guy at the grad party that had held Sara's attention. And it was not Ben.

Then before Carrie knew it, Sara was pulling into the Disney's Grand Floridian Resort & Spa. The parking lot located in front of the entrance made for an easy walk to the motel.

After checking in, they went to their room and unpacked, which didn't take long since they only planned to spend one night.

"Okay, we can grab the monorail on the second floor." Sara smiled.

"Let the fun begin." Carrie pulled on her backpack. "I love Disney World."

Sara laughed. "You've always been a kid at heart."

Carrie nodded. "Been to Disney lots of times and I never get tired of it."

"I know, right?"

After passing through security, they hopped on the monorail and rode three minutes to Magic Kingdom.

"Listen." Sara raised a brow. "I love that music. It's so magical."

Carrie nodded. *When You Wish Upon A Star* rang out while they strolled the avenue.

She loved Main Street, lined with shops selling merchandise and food. The décor was early 20th century small-town America and provided the best combination of attractions, restaurants, and shows for all ages.

They continued down Main Street and made a stop at a town square setting, complete with a flagpole, train station, and ice cream parlor. Carrie felt as though she'd stepped back in time.

By late-morning, they found themselves in the middle of Liberty Square when Sara stopped mid-sidewalk.

"I've got to get a turkey leg," Sara blurted.

Carrie saw enthusiasm wash across her friend's features.

"Oh that's an affirmative." Carrie's mouth

watered. She couldn't help herself, she'd never been able to pass up a Disney's turkey leg which was nothing like Thanksgiving turkey. It was smoked and tasted more like ham than turkey. So savory and juicy. "Do you want to share one?"

"Uh huh. I love them, but I could never manage a whole one."

When they walked into Liberty Square Market, spicy aromas wafted throughout the store, making Carrie's stomach rumble. Like she expected, with Disney's turkey legs such a popular item, they had to wait in a long line.

"One turkey leg, please." Carrie stepped up to the counter. "And could we have paper plates and forks?"

"Certainly." The clerk behind the counter nodded.

The clerk's expression told Carrie this was not an unusual request. Most people would have trouble finishing off an entire leg.

When they finished the tasty morsel, they spent most of the afternoon checking out several different attractions before they boarded the 16-minute Pirates of the Caribbean ride. Bypassing the first row, they found two empty seats in row two. When a couple plopped down in front of them, Carrie looked at Sara and laughed. She knew from experience sitting in the front row of the vehicle guaranteed getting splashed at the first drop.

Space Mountain was the last stop of the day before heading to the resort for a late dinner on the tiered outside deck. The Grand Floridian Resort provided great views of the Magic Kingdom; the proximity meant they were close enough to get a good view of the fireworks over Cinderella Castle. Carrie never wanted to miss Disney's grand days-end finale.

"What's on the agenda for tomorrow?" Carrie yawned, then looked at her watch.

"Epcot?"

"That's good for me."

"Let's sleep in tomorrow. No need to get there at the crack of dawn like we did this morning."

"I agree. If we sleep till noon, who's gonna care?" Carrie chuckled. "This is our time."

"You had a good time today, right?"

"The best. Thank you for suggesting this trip."

CHAPTER TWENTY-EIGHT

Saturday when Carrie woke up, sunlight streamed into the room. She squinted and blinked to get her bearings. The TV displayed an Infomercial with the volume low. Her mouth opened wide in a yawn, and she realized she'd slept on the sofa all night.

Too wired and unable to fall asleep the previous evening, she'd popped out of bed, headed to the kitchen, poured a glass of milk, then curled up on the couch to watch an old movie. She had no idea when she'd dozed off but could not recall the end of the movie.

She eased herself into a sitting position and discovered her neck and back were cramped up, and she did not feel rested. While she sat for a moment, massaging the back of her neck, letting the muscles stretch out, the stiffness eased. She swung her legs off the couch and put her feet on the floor, then searched for her slippers with her bare toes. Routine. That's what she'd become accustomed to. Just get through 24 hours at a time.

And the days had flown by but she'd not talked to Kent yet. The opportune time never seemed to happen. Carrie occupied her time with work and family, but she hated watching the worry lines crease the faces of her loved ones when she was around them.

Well today would be different. She would spend the day at the beach with Brenda and her husband, Carl. When Brenda had invited her, at first she'd declined. She didn't want to be the fifth wheel. But Brenda had assured her they'd have fun.

When Carl's white SUV pulled into her apartment's parking lot, Carrie grabbed her bag and sped through the doorway. After locking the door behind her, she stood in front of the vehicle before they'd had a chance to honk.

"You must have been watching for us," Brenda said.

"I was. Can't help myself, I'm always up and ready way before time to go."

"Same here." Carl glanced over his shoulder and rolled his eyes. "I'm really looking forward to today."

Carrie laughed. "I take it you're not much of an oceanfront fan."

"Once a year is plenty for me."

"I love going to the beach." Carrie leaned into the comfy seat. "I haven't done it much this year though."

"Me, too." Brenda playfully poked her husband's arm. "But not a fan of going by myself."

"Same here." Carrie totally agreed. Occasionally it felt relaxing but could soon turn to boredom.

"My hubby will spend the day, first looking for shells, then finding an umbrella under a palm tree in the shade and nap the afternoon away. He's not the height of fun on a beach date."

"Hey, don't complain." Carl laughed. "How much fun do you think you are at a football game?"

"Touche."

Carrie enjoyed the easy banter between the couple while Carl drove the 45 minutes to Clearwater Beach. They'd been married 22 years according to Brenda, and it was obvious they still had a good time together. How she longed for that experience. To have a partner that would stay by her side for nearly a quarter of a century seemed unattainable.

When Carl pulled the SUV into the North Beach Parking Plaza, Carrie grabbed her bag and asked, "How much are the tickets?"

Four dollars each, and I've got it." Carl smiled

"Okay. But I'll pay for a cabana, beach chairs and umbrellas," Carrie offered.

"Not with me around." Carl winked.

The three found an empty area close to the water and chose loungers not in use. When Carl eyed the cabana, Carrie smiled. He'd most likely nab that very soon.

Carrie pulled in a breath while she scanned the stunning beach with its white sugary sands and emerald waters located just steps from hotels and restaurants. The sun emerged from a screen of cirrus clouds, glittering briefly on the water. Clearwater Beach remained one of her favorite spots to spend a day relaxing.

She eyed the bay's shoreline, which was an endless slow curve with beautiful blue water lapping against the beach. The waves rippled in striations of dark blue and black, and a balmy breeze, smelling fresh and salty, caressed her hair.

The sight sent her back in time, and she found herself remembering her family spending endless days basking in the sun, enjoying the beach, and most of all each other. Where had the time gone? Now they stayed so busy with their personal lives, there was barely enough time to get everyone together every few months.

Suddenly a majestic blue heron flew overhead, flapping its angular wings, leading with its long neck, graceful and strong, the hue of heaven itself.

Tears stung her eyes. She took the heron as a sign. It resonated within her. It felt like Kent's soul, beautiful, strong, and proud, taking flight. Out of her life.

Carrie settled into a chair beside Brenda, slid out of her flip-flops, then scrunched her toes in the powdery white sand. The seagulls overhead called out with crying squawks, begging for just one morsel of food. She enjoyed the laid-back gulf-coast experience with consistently calm surf conditions. She leaned back in the chair and closed her eyes. The murmuring of the waves felt hypnotic, oozing onto the beach and somehow brought Kent forefront in her head yet again. Her mind conjured up the

CEO's handsome face, and she got lost in memories of their time together. The touch of his lips pressing on hers washed over her, and her heart swelled until she was certain it would burst.

"Let's go in for a dip," Brenda said.

Her friend's words brought Carrie back to the present, and she shook off the man who had crushed her.

Carrie jumped to her feet. "I'm in."

Brenda pulled her beach cover over her head. "I need a cool-down."

Carrie followed suit, slipped her cover-up off and trailed behind her friend to the water's edge. She looked back toward the chairs and noticed Carl had already found a spot in the cabana.

Carrie watched Brenda dive into a wave, the warm Gulf water embracing her like a hug. While her friend swam farther out, Carrie waded calf deep in the water. When a larger wave headed her way, she'd turn and follow it to shore. Then repeat.

Brenda was much more enthused with swimming in the ocean. Carrie liked to be around the water, and on the water, but not necessarily in the water.

An admitted people-watcher, Carrie noticed a couple strolling along the pier. A man and a woman, not too far out, but far enough she could only make out their outlines on the dock. They walked hand-in-hand, probably to steady one another in the wind while they ventured farther out. And then suddenly they turned and backtracked, walking quickly through the sand to a car parked in the adjoining lot. When they reached the pavement, they stomped their feet a few times, apparently trying to shake off the accumulated sand.

It was only after she watched the black car spin out of the lot that she noticed the woman walking back toward the beach, her feet dragging through the sand, deliberate and lazy, as one does when they're thinking about something else and not at all about the beach. It was obvious she was crying. Her head hung low, and her hands clutched a beach bag.

The woman headed right toward her and nearly collided with Carrie. Carrie held out a hand to steady the lady's gait. She was pretty, from her wavy chestnut tresses and lush lips down to a very nice figure. Her expressive hazel eyes were striking, even though puffy from apparent crying.

"Oh, I'm sorry. Wasn't looking. I'm such a klutz."

"No problem. Are you okay?"

No, I'm terrible. This is the worst day of my life." She swiped a hand across her red and swollen eyes. "I just got dumped."

Join the crowd, Carrie thought, but held her tongue.

"Why are men such slugs?"

Carrie shrugged. "That's a question I keep asking myself."

"I thought everything was great between us. Even today, on the beach. We were having a good time, or so I thought. Then when we head back to his car, he told me he'd found someone else. Didn't want to hurt me, but didn't want anything more to do with me."

"He took off and just left you stranded?" Carrie flashed on a time when she'd been fed the same cruel brush-off.

"No, he said he was going to take me home. But my heart couldn't take being in the same car with him. I've got friends I can call."

"I know what you're going through. I've been dumped. Not just once. Twice. It hurts."

"Yes, it does."

Understanding passed over the stranger's features, and she dropped her head into her hands and cried audibly.

"Do you live around here? In Clearwater? I live in Tampa. I would be happy to meet you for coffee sometime, that is, if you need someone to talk to." Carrie laid a hand on her arm and said, "My name is Carrie Dennison."

The woman's head shot up and her eyes grew wide as saucers. "You have got to be kidding me?"

"Huh. . ." The woman's reaction confused Carrie.

"My fiancé that dumped me. . ." The woman's tears turned to a sardonic laugh. "His name is Jeff."

"No way." Carrie pulled in a sharp breath, then forced it out through pursed lips. She tried to hold on to her sanity. But that was hard to do. The irony was unbelievable. "So, you're Connie?" Jeff had left her for this woman. Now he'd just dumped her.

"Yep. That's me."

The two women exchanged glances that were an eyelash shy of contempt.

"Way to go Jeff." Carrie couldn't keep the sarcasm from slicing through her voice.

"I hope you know, I never meant to hurt you."

"Don't worry about it."

"I was already head over heels in love with him before I even knew you existed. Much less that he was in a relationship with you."

"I'm over him. It took a while, but he's out of my system. For good."

Connie's eyes filled with tears again and spilled over. "I'm sure you think I'm getting what I deserve."

"No, not at all. It's a shame he's fooled someone else."

"You're a better woman than me. If it was reversed, I'd be laughing my head off."

"Well, I am sorry." It no longer mattered to Carrie that Connie had been her nemesis. It didn't matter anymore that he had cheated on her. "You don't deserve what Jeff did to you."

"He's already hooked up with someone else. No telling how long he's been seeing her behind my back."

In a matter of a couple seconds, raw truth slid across Carrie's mind. Jeff had still been with Connie when he'd tracked her down in the hospital and tried to lure her back. He'd told Carrie, he'd been dumped. But the truth be told, it was the other way around. He was getting ready to dump Connie. What a loser.

With new-found determination that slammed through her body like a punch from a seasoned wrestler, she made a vow right on the spot. She'd not be fooled by another man. Never again.

"Hey, I'm starved. Let's go eat." Brenda hustled through the sand. "Oops, am I interrupting?"

Connie jumped up and brushed sand from her

legs. "No. Not at all. I was just leaving."

A puzzled look slid across Brenda's face. "Please don't let me run you off."

"No problem. I need to go."

"You're welcome to grab a bite of lunch with us." Carrie stood. "This is my good friend, Brenda…"

Before Carrie could continue, Connie nodded toward Brenda, then shuffled down the beach.

"What was that about?"

"You'll never believe me." Carrie chuckled. "I'll explain over lunch."

Brenda tossed her a curious look, bent down, retrieved her cell, and obviously sent a text.

"I'll see if Carl wants to join us," Brenda said.

Carrie slipped into her cover-up, then heard her friend's phone ping.

Brenda looked at her cell. "He's already eating a hot dog in the cabana."

Carrie laughed. "He cracks me up."

"He's such a dud on a beach date."

They headed to Frenchy's Rockaway Grill, right on the sand. No need to change out of swimwear, come straight from the beach was their motto. The popular eatery, already hopping with the lunchtime crowd, reeked with the smell of warm, fresh bread, making Carrie's mouth water.

Just then the hostess approached. "Table for two?"

"Yes." Carrie's eyes scanned the packed dining area. "Hope there's a table available."

The hostess nodded, then her lips turned up at

the corners. "There is. Right this way."

When they were seated, the hostess placed menus in front of them and only a couple of minutes passed before the waiter appeared and took their drink and meal orders.

"Okay, Carrie, tell me who that was with you on the beach."

"Okay, but I warn you, you're not going to believe this."

"All right, already. Out with it."

"Her name is Connie. She just got dumped."

Brenda's perfectly plucked eyebrows shot up. She tapped her fingers on the table. "Is that the unbelievable part?"

"Nope." Carrie shook her head. "She got dumped by Jeff."

"The Jeff that you used to date?"

"One and the same."

Brenda blinked, then ran a slender hand through her unruly hair. "Is that freaky or what?"

The waiter brought two sweet teas, placed them on the table, then walked away.

"How come she was telling you her tales of woe?"

Carrie picked up her glass, took a small sip of tea. "After he dumped her, she refused to let him take her home. She wandered down the sand, crying, and nearly ran into me."

"Talk about the coincidence of all times."

"I know, right?"

"Did she know Jeff was your ex?"

"Didn't have a clue. And I didn't know it was Jeff that had dumped her until I introduced myself and she nearly choked."

The waiter returned, placed two BLTs with sides of coleslaw on the table, then asked, "Can I get you anything else?"

"No, thank you." Carrie looked at her friend, who shook her head no.

"So what were they doing on the beach?"

"She thought it was just a date. Didn't have a clue she was about to get axed." Carrie put her fork down and made eye contact with her friend.

"You're kidding."

"I'm not." Carrie dropped her voice to a whisper and leaned in. "I could see them on the pier, too far away to recognize Jeff. But close enough to see they looked lovey dovey. Kissing and cuddling."

"Wow. Strange."

"She said everything seemed to be just fine between them. Jeff had not given her the slightest inclination there was a problem. Then on the way to his car, he told her he'd found someone else."

"That man has to be narcissistic!"

"He's definitely self-absorbed."

They finished the sandwiches and ordered dessert and coffee.

"Her story confirmed my decision to avoid men." Carrie cleared her throat.

"Ahh, not all guys are losers."

"No?" Carrie laughed, but it lacked any humor. "Just the ones I pick?"

"That's just a total of two. There are lots of other guys out there that would be very lucky to latch onto you."

"You do realize when Jeff approached me in the

cafeteria he was still with Connie. And he'd already hooked up with another woman."

"I agree he is the scum of the earth."

When the waiter set desserts and coffees on the table and walked away, Carrie's stomach turned into jelly. The coffee smelled strong and bold just like she liked it, and Frenchy's always made a great cup, but today it didn't appeal. The giant piece of tiramisu, her favorite dessert in the world, might as well have been a pile of bacon grease.

"It's okay if you can't eat anymore right now," Brenda said. "Take it to go."

Carrie scrubbed her face with her hands. "When I think of what Jeff did and compare the similarity to what Kent's done, it makes me physically sick."

"I know. And I hate what you're going through, and it's a lot more than today's encounter."

Carrie continued to stare at her dessert. She scraped the cocoa from the top of the whipped cream.

Brenda, of all her friends, understood her difficulty in articulating her troubles. She was so much like Dad in that aspect. But that still didn't make it any easier to come out with it. "What makes you think there's something else?"

"Because I don't think running into Connie made you so upset you just look at your dessert," Brenda said. "Did something else happen with Kent?"

Carrie rolled her eyes, but secretly she was amazed at how Brenda read her mind. "No. That's over. Whatever that was." She made air quotes.

"What is it then?"

"Something is wrong with me."

"No, there isn't."

"There's got to be."

"Like what?"

"I feel I'm not good enough to have a man love me. I can't seem to hold a man's attention for very long, must less have them love me long term. I'm afraid I'm doomed to a lonely, loveless life."

"That is utter nonsense. You have just had some rotten luck. Mr. Right will come along. Just you wait and see. I know you are destined to be loved."

CHAPTER TWENTY-NINE

When Carrie completed the afternoon rounds, she headed to the nurse's station where Brenda stood. Her friend's eyes were locked on the iPad she held in her hand.

"Don't tell me, we've got a new admission," Carrie said.

Brenda shook her head. "Not for us yet. An emergency ruptured appendix was just sent to OR."

"Night shift's admission for sure."

Brenda nodded. "So go ahead and take a break, Carrie." Her friend shooed her off with a wave of her hand.

"Okay. I'll be back in fifteen."

"Don't rush. I'll cover for you."

Carrie stepped off the elevator, then walked into the little gift shop on the first floor of the hospital.

She purchased a hot chocolate, then roamed aimlessly through the nick-knacks, not looking for anything, just biding her time. She took a sip from the cocoa, and it reminded her how much better Kent's brew tasted and what good times they'd shared in his kitchen. Would she never quit thinking about that man?

She had promised her family she would talk to Kent, but she didn't want to show up at his apartment unexpected. It would feel awkward for her to say the least. Plus she didn't want to embarrass him or herself. She wished she'd never agreed to talk to him because she wasn't ready to hear him say the dreaded words, 'I've found someone else'. She shook her head and took another drink from the Styrofoam cup.

"We need to talk." A voice startled her.

Kent's tone, soft and low, was for her ears only. And she felt those four words like soft puffs of air against her hair. His musky and citrusy scent, raw and noble, wafted over her.

Her throat went dry and she swallowed hard. Her palms felt clammy when she met his gaze and tried not to pay any extra attention to how close his mouth was from her face. "About what?" Her voice was barely a whisper.

"About what Brenda thought she saw. . ."

A chill slithered up her spine while his startling words messed with her heart. She'd been on the verge of seeking him out to talk about the same thing. Now he'd initiated the discussion.

She felt Kent looking at her, and a strange emotion lurked behind his blue eyes. He was probably waiting for her to say something but she remained silent.

"We need to talk and we need some privacy. Anything that bothers you matters to me and I want to hear about it face to face."

"Okay."

"Will you meet me at Scooters after work?"

"Yes," she answered. But would she? Was she ready for the confrontation?

Odd he'd opted to meet at Scooters rather than Starbucks. He couldn't know it was her favorite coffee shop. Could he? They'd never discussed it. Had he picked a spot she liked to let her down gently? For the longest moment she remained suspended in time, picturing how she'd act, what she'd say when he owned up to what he'd done. She was at a loss, thinking she'd never bounce back from this because she feared her heart would refuse to function anymore.

He gave his head a quick jerk in the direction of the exit. "Meet me there at six?"

Carrie nodded. She watched him turn on his heel and walk through the gift shop doorway. Then she took one last drink and tossed the cup in the trash.

Back at the nurse's station, she opened her PC, entered her passcode, and checked the TGH EpicLink, a real-time, secure web access to her patient's medical records. Satisfied all remained well with the ones under her care, she checked the incoming patient list. One due before shift change. Time to get busy she told herself. No time to dwell on Kent.

"You're back." Brenda rounded the corner with

an IV set-up in her hand. "Can you help me with this? Ms. Braxton, age 22, post bone transplant, is freaking out because we need to start more fluids."

"Freaking out or scared?" Carrie knew the generation Zs valued self-care and were more likely to question rules and authority because they were used to finding what they needed on their own. But often they didn't know what they needed, especially in a new setting. She would bet Ms. Braxton thought she no longer needed IV fluids.

"A little of both. You are closer to her age, I'm sure she'll feel more at ease with you starting the IV. And she wants to be called by her given name, Annie."

"Let's do it."

When Carrie and her supervisor entered the young lady's room, Carrie saw Annie tapping on her phone.

"Hey, Annie, I hear you aren't too wild about having your IV replaced."

"I don't need it anymore. They took it out in Recovery." She pointed to her over-bed table where a half-empty water container set. "Look how much I've already gotten down."

"Good job. We want you to drink lots. But the reason we want the IV going is two-fold. One, there are electrolytes in the solution. And two, we need to keep a vein open for your antibiotics and any other medication your physician might prescribe. If you do well, the IV will be gone for good maybe as early as tomorrow."

Annie screwed her mouth to the side.

Carrie nodded for Brenda to hang the bag of

solution while Carrie opened the tubing.

"Let's see what kind of veins you have, Annie."

"I have huge veins." She held out an arm for Carrie to see.

"Yes, you do. This will just take a couple minutes then you can get back to texting."

Annie squeezed her eyes shut and bit down on her bottom lip.

Carrie had no trouble starting the IV. "You can open your eyes, Annie. I'm all done."

Annie grinned, then picked up her phone.

"Use your call light if you need anything." Carrie handed her the apparatus. "This is for the TV. . ."

Annie threw up a hand. "I know. I know how to use it."

"I'm sure you do." Just like a Gen Z, Carrie thought and gave the young lady a smile.

Satisfied she managed to start the IV without incident, Carrie left Annie's room.

The minutes ticked by, and Carrie checked her smart watch frequently. Finally it was time to clock out. A sudden chill crawled up her spine, making her tremble. Why had she agreed to meet Kent? What good would it do? The final goodbye, she thought and sighed.

Being in control was Carrie's forte, and she felt she'd ventured way out of her comfort zone. So used to finding what she needed on her own, she wondered if she'd fallen into the same Gen Z pragmatic mind-set as Annie.

* * *

Several vehicles were lined up at the take-out window at Scooters when Carrie turned her car into the lot and found a parking spot. The proximity made it a favorite hang-out, not only for the hospital employees, but also downtown Tampa businesses. She hoped the coffee shop wouldn't be quite as busy as the take-out window.

It wasn't. The sun hiding behind a cloud, made it darker outside than inside the coffee shop. She could see right in, into the industrial designed space with its bold, finished look, the cute little tables, the recycled things that hung from the ceiling. Taking in his blond hair, Carrie spotted Kent through the window before she entered.

He was waiting for her. The second Carrie walked into Scooters, Kent closed the door behind her, then took her arm and guided her to the counter where they ordered cappuccinos. Carrie couldn't help but notice how the girl behind the counter looked hungrily at Kent. How her eyes flirted with him. It wasn't her fault, Carrie got that, and yet it didn't make her dislike it any less. Of course women of all ages would give their birthright to have him. Why had she even considered they'd have a monogamous relationship? There would always be someone waiting in the sidelines to hook the handsome CEO. She focused on the counter while the hostess prepared their order.

After they had their drinks in tow, they found a seat toward the back that faced the street, and for a lack of anything else to say Carrie said, "Private, yet comfortable."

"I think that's what we need."

"You think?" Carrie avoided his gaze. It was hard to look into the eyes of the person who planned to shatter her life. Not that he hadn't already accomplished that, he had. But she guessed this little get together was to officially end whatever they'd had.

"Yes, I think. We have a lot to talk about."

Carrie pulled her eyes from the window and rested them on Kent. She rearranged herself in the plush leather seat, and for a nanosecond his familiar and overwhelming smile almost got to her. Almost.

"I love the cappuccino here." Kent ran a hand through his windblown hair and settled back.

She watched him take a careful sip from the cup, then place it gently on the table.

Carrie's heart skipped a beat. She couldn't wait any longer for the let-down. She cleared her throat. "Okay, I'll bite. Tell me what you think Brenda witnessed?"

"The woman Brenda saw in my office. Her name is Ellen."

Carrie felt herself flinch.

Kent lifted his hands, palms up. "She kissed me, Carrie. A totally uninvited kiss. It threw me completely off balance. If Brenda would have hung around a second longer, she would've seen me push her away."

"You have to be kidding." Carrie shot him a disbelieving look. "Brenda said she learned 'Ellen' had visited your office on several occasions." Carrie made air quotes when she said the woman's name.

"That's true. But I swear to you, I didn't encourage those visits. I didn't want them. If I'm lying, may lightning strike me right now." He took another swig from his cup and smiled. "See? I'm still sitting here, unharmed."

Carrie couldn't help but smile.

"I met her at the hospital where I worked in Kansas City. I liked her okay, and when she asked me to join her for dinner, I went. Big mistake." Kent rotated the mug between both hands. "I had a good enough time with her. She's smart, funny and easy to talk to. But I never, not for one minute, wanted anything more than friendship with her."

"How long did you two date?

"Four or five times."

"Who broke it off?"

"I did." Kent shifted in his chair, and she saw torment slide across his eyes. He continued, "She wanted more than I could give her. I had told her more than once, I was not interested in forming a serious relationship with her, but she wasn't having it. After our last date, she asked me to join her in her apartment. When I refused, she went off. Calling me a user was one of the milder words she threw at me."

"She sounds a little manic."

Kent nodded. "I agree. When I made it plain I would never go out with her again, she tried to cause trouble with me at the hospital."

"It must have been hard trying to deal with her drama."

When Kent reached across the table and absently played with her fingers, the soft caresses of his skin against hers caused tingles to crawl up her arm.

"I realize now I should never have agreed to

even one dinner date with her."

"We all make choices we later regret."

"She told me I was throwing my life away and said I'd never find anyone else like her. She threatened to make my life miserable."

"Sounds kinda scary."

"To be honest, her actions did scare me. At the time, I wouldn't have put anything past her."

"So did she finally back off. . . that is until she showed up here?"

"By the time I nabbed the position at Tampa General, I thought she was over her obsession with me. That's what I get for thinking. One day, out of the blue, she shows up in my office. Same old obsession driving her."

Carrie bit her lower lip. "I'm sorry I was so quick to jump to conclusions."

"No problem. I can only imagine how it looked when Brenda saw us together."

"Please believe me, Brenda was not trying to cause you grief. She was just worried about me."

"I completely understand." Kent rubbed his forehead. "I have alerted security. If she comes anywhere near my office again, I'll have them intervene. She's obviously not going to pay attention to anything I tell her."

Carrie nodded. Silence fell like dusk and hung between them like an elephant in the room.

"Is something else going on?" Carrie braced herself. Everything seemed good a minute ago, but now. . .What?

"Carrie, I saw you in the cafeteria last month kissing some guy."

Carrie could not stop herself. She laughed. "You aren't going to believe this." She shook her head, laughed some more.

Kent obviously didn't seem to find anything amusing, so she pulled in a calming breath, blew it out slowly, and composed herself.

She turned in the seat, angled her body toward him. "Since we're clearing the air, I'll be honest with you. Believe it or not, something similar happened to me."

"Whatever you want to tell me, I'm ready to talk about it." He paused and swallowed. "Give it to me straight."

Simple. Frank. To the point. She liked that about him. Somehow she knew she could trust this man with her heart.

"My ex, Jeff, showed up unexpectedly in the cafeteria. He pleaded with me to come back to him."

Kent's brows shot up an inch. "I hope you're gonna tell me you blew him off."

Carrie nodded. "That I did."

Kent wiped a hand across his head, then shook his fingers as if he were wiping sweat from his brow.

Carrie laughed. She loved Kent's dramatics.

"There was a time in my life I would have jumped at the chance to go back to him. But when I came face to face with him in the cafeteria, I knew I had no lingering feelings left for him. I told him I didn't have the least desire to renew a relationship with him."

Their gazes connected, and a familiar heat raced

to her cheeks. Ironic how a simple look turned her inside out.

Carrie shared her encounter with Connie at the beach, then said, "The guy I had been so in love with dumped me for another woman. Then he dumped that woman for another woman."

"And you thought history was repeating itself with me?'

Carrie nodded. "I did."

"You were hurt. And I'm sorry I caused any of that pain."

When he snatched her hand and brought it to his chest, she pulled in a long breath and slowly released it. His touch so warm and firm, so full of promises. All the things she'd ever dreamed of but was afraid she'd never obtain.

"I want your heart, Carrie. I want it for myself, just like I've given you mine."

Carrie hadn't thought one could be petrified by pure, sheer joy. It never seemed possible. But she sat across from him as he laid his heart in her hands, and all she could do was stare at him with a thousand unsaid words stuck on the tip of her tongue.

Kent released her hand, leaned forward. "I would never cheat on you, Carrie. And you can bet your life, I will never walk away from you."

She started to speak, but the words stuck in her throat.

She saw something flash across Kent's face. The space between their mouths crackled with electricity, and the flutter in her stomach morphed to butterflies of excitement.

"Carrie, you have this fire that burns inside you, and it illuminates the world around you. You are light. And passionate. Your laughter alone can lift my mood and turn my day around in a matter of seconds. You can light up entire rooms. And it's because of all these different things that make you who you are."

Carrie's heart thrashed against the cavity of her chest with a wildness she'd never experienced. What a wonderful man, she thought. He kept showing her how perfect he was. He kept unveiling all those beautiful parts of him that made her giddy and dizzy. His words were, without a doubt in her mind, the most beautiful things she would ever hear said about her. To her. And for her.

"Carrie, don't you know by now I am in love with you?"

With sudden swiftness, his words attacked Carrie's mind. She sucked in a quick breath and felt her eyes go wide. Her whole world exploded with happiness. When he slid his hands across the table and took both her hands in his, Carrie felt the love flow from him through her entire body. Her eyes closed, and for an instant, the floor seemed to dissolve under her.

"I've never loved anyone like I love you. From that first day when the dog bowled you over, I knew I'd never be the same. When I looked down into your beautiful face, I knew you were the one."

He let go with one hand, reached into his coat pocket and pulled out a velvet box. As though he'd practiced for this moment, he opened it in a single move. There inside lay a diamond ring bigger than any Carrie had ever seen.

He stood then fell to one knee right in the middle of Scooters. "Will you do me the honor of being my wife?"

"I love you. I'm in love with you. Yes, yes, yes. I will marry you." She fumbled for words, just like she did in the early stages with him. But somehow it didn't matter. He loved her. Really loved her for who she was.

The customers in Scooters applauded. Carrie didn't even blush. She was too overcome with Kent's presence and his love, there was no need for embarrassment. When the patrons turned back to their own business, Kent stood.

He lifted Carrie up from the seat. "It's you and me. My love. My whole world."

He gathered her in his arms with a tenderness, a reverence that left her breathless. She felt his lips claim hers, and she basked in the newly found confidence that flooded through her soul; and she knew, no doubt about it, she was destined to trust in love.

ABOUT THE AUTHOR

Born in Arkansas, Lois Curran spent most of her childhood in Salem, Oregon before her family moved to Lebanon, Missouri when she was fifteen. She now considers the Ozarks her home.

Her debut novel, Destined to Love Again, is the first in a trilogy of Contemporary Christian Romance. She also writes Suspense/Thrillers.

An avid reader, writing has always been a passion. Lois decided to become a full-time writer after she retired from her position as Director of Nursing at her local health department. As a Registered Nurse, she uses real world details to create believable characters.

Cruising and traveling are high on Curran's list of favorite things to do. She also enjoys taking pictures of her family and friends and sharing them on social media. She spends the remainder of her time doing what she loves best – writing.

Curran is a member of Ozarks Romance Authors, Sleuths' Ink Mystery Writers, and American Christian Fiction Writers.